E. Lynn Linton

Through the Long Night

Vol. II

E. Lynn Linton

Through the Long Night
Vol. II

ISBN/EAN: 9783337213022

Printed in Europe, USA, Canada, Australia, Japan

Cover: Foto ©Andreas Hilbeck / pixelio.de

More available books at **www.hansebooks.com**

THROUGH THE LONG NIGHT.

VOL. II.

THROUGH

THE LONG NIGHT

BY

E. LYNN LINTON

AUTHOR OF

'PATRICIA KEMBALL,' 'THE ATONEMENT OF LEAM DUNDAS,'
'IONE,' 'PASTON CAREW,' ETC.

IN THREE VOLUMES.

VOL. II.

LONDON:

HURST AND BLACKETT, LIMITED,
13, GREAT MARLBOROUGH STREET.

CONTENTS

OF

THE SECOND VOLUME.

***

BOOK THE SECOND.

(CONTINUED.)

MIDNIGHT.

BOOK THE SECOND.

(CONTINUED.)

THROUGH THE LONG NIGHT.

CHAPTER II.

THE UNEXPÉCTED VISITOR.

WAS it from ignorance or design that Anthony Harford dispensed with the formalities usual among civilized people, as touching guest and host, and set out for Hindfleet without notice given or time appointed? Even proud folk sometimes condescend to small ruses; and Anthony, though prouder than most, had thus condescended.

He wanted to take his old friends unawares, so that he might test them by that most trustworthy of all personal litmus-papers—surprise. To give time for preparation was to offer a premium for pretence; which was exactly what he did not wish. Since his return to England he had been fanning the embers of his half-extinct memories, cherishing touching sentiments and forming dainty pictures of his old friend and pretty plaything; and he wanted to see how he should be received when the stage was not set nor were the lamps trimmed for his reception. It was the old parable of The Virgins. Had the Asplines preserved their oil of affection for him, or had they wasted it?

Such ties as Anthony might have had out there in the Wild West—such loves as might have brightened his life and softened the ruggedness of his self-elected path—were either buried beneath the church-yard clay, or had been washed away by some great tidal wave of change—estrangement—who knows what? In any case, there was no reason why he should not give his thoughts, his dreams, his fancies to Anne Aspline, or to any other. And in truth he was in the mood which makes what is called a 'marrying man,'—ready to fall in love with the first likely girl who presented herself.

Hence it was that, shortly after the interchange of those formal business letters, he packed up his portmanteau—so far as he had gone yet, he disdained a man for his own personal service—and took the train to Kingshouse, driving up to Hindfleet unheralded, uninvited, unexpected.

It was a dull winter's day, and the brief twilight was stealing on like a dusky web woven between sky and earth. The untenanted and sodden fields, with their patches of dirty snow left in the lee of the hedges and their trees standing like gaunt skeletons in the blank expanse, looked all the more desolate for the failure of such dull light as the day had given, and for the gathering gloom of the coming darkness. Heavy snow had fallen about a week since, but now the thaw had reduced everything to mud and ruin and the sense of an underground sea stagnating beneath the earth. It was one of those typical English days which give foreigners cause to blaspheme and which chill the very marrow of the stalwart natives themselves—a day when animals huddle together in piteous dejection for mutual warmth—when no birds are to be seen, save crows and sparrows, and sea-birds driven inland—when men are morose, and hard drinkers drink heavily—when women are tearful or shrill-tongued according to their pattern, and when even the children do not laugh—when joy, good luck, the hope of the future and the beauty of the past are all dead alike, and nothing is left save the direful gloom of a universal charnel-house.

The whole scene, like the atmosphere, was so unutterably dispiriting that Anthony mentally wondered if the game were worth the candle, while he muttered into his damp beard a few objurgations of an American complexion, and drew his fur-lined coat more closely over his broad chest. These six miles between Hindfleet and the Kingshouse station seemed as if they would never come to an end—as if that interesting question touching the candle and the game would never be answered. The way was like the Irishman's, whereof the end has been cut off; and Hindfleet was surely to be found only in the moon!

At last they made the lane which was so

picturesque in summer, but which to-day was a mere way of slush and wreck, and, turning sharply to the right, came to the lodge gates of a well-kept place, which the driver said briefly was Hindfleet.

'At last?' said Anthony, with a certain grim humour, which the driver resented as a reflection on his broken-kneed and broken-winded beast— to his mind quite as good as any reasonable man could expect at such a place as Kingshouse. And if gentlemen wanted blood horses for their carriages on such a day as this, they had better bring them along with them by train, he said shortly, while he stood stolidly by the poor jaded brute's drooping head, as though he would run away at the first chance, and was as bad to hold as if his sire had been Bucephalus.

The servants were just beginning to close the shutters and light up the house as Anthony entered. Already the hall was a-glow with light and warmth. The freshly-trimmed fire was blazing in the open grate. The large Gothic lanthorn was like a sun swinging in chains from the ceiling. Coming out of the dimness of the outer air

it struck on Anthony with a delightful sense of
welcome, and was, as it were, the keynote of the
whole harmony. His eye caught one or two
things which he remembered, and which carried
him back to his long past years. How familiar
they looked!   That otter—that 'salmo ferox,'—
those ptarmigan, male and female, poor hapless
lovers!—the long-legged heron and the round-
eyed horned owl—the slender-bodied weasel and
the brilliantly plumaged king-fisher—each in its
respective case, duly labelled and inventoried—
why, it seemed only yesterday that he had looked
at them with a boy's longing to capture their
like, when he, too, should be able to tabulate
places and dates, and blazon himself as the
plucky sportsman whose bag was worth arsenic
and glass.

While he was taking off his coat, paying the
man, and giving curt directions about his portmanteau—which he called a valise—his mind
went in parallel lines, and the past and present
were equally distinct. He was sincerely moved,
and prepared for an unwonted amount of
enthusiasm. His American reserve had melted

as frost beneath the breath of the south wind.
His caution had gone with his reserve. Hindfleet
would be to him what the old Hall had been—
his home ; and the Asplines would be as his own.
But while this rush of friendly sentiment was
sweeping through his heart, Mrs. Aspline, in the
drawing-room, looked at her daughter with dis-
may, and whispered in a voice of conventional
horror :

'Anne, I do verily believe that creature has
come unannounced. Who on earth else would
call on such a horrid evening as this, and be
such a long time in the hall? What a fool he
must be ! My word !'

'Surely not,' said Anne, with a slight flutter
at her heart; for all her denial, feeling very certain that it was Anthony Harford and none other
whose voice and feet filled the hall with such
plenitude of masculine vigour.

And then, conjecture was ended by the servant
opening the door, and 'Mr. Harford' coming
from the light of the hall into the semi-darkness
of the room.

'You see, I took you at your word, and came

right away without further notice,' said a richly toned voice with an unmistakable American accent—a voice in which, for all its richness of tone, however, no play of feeling of any kind was to be detected. It stated a fact, it did not express an emotion; but it seemed also to make sure of a response.

Both ladies rose from their chairs and went forward to meet their visitor. How stout dear old Cookey had grown! She was like one of her own butter-tubs set on feet. And how slender that round little puff-ball looked, out-lined against the fire which touched the edges of her dress and figure with a kind of fiery glow —half-flame, half-colour!

'Why, here you are, just as in old times, and I am right glad to see you again!' he added, meeting them with both hands held out.

Mrs. Aspline had intended to be properly dignified, as became a lady a little offended by a liberty and stiffened by long absence; but hospitality conquered temper, and she greeted Anthony as warmly as if he had been the old friend expected and desired of his dreams. Her

dignity dropped to her feet like a veil unpinned ;
while Anne, who had intended to be sweetly
patronizing—perhaps even affectionate, in a
superior, sisterly kind of way—was suddenly
reduced to a state of embarrassment which made
her appear as hard as a wooden doll and as cold
as an ice-maiden. This was not the man to
patronize, instruct, reform, rescue—this man who
stood before her as a king and made her feel as
small as the child he remembered. She was so
completely taken aback by this sudden shifting
of the wind—she was so embarrassed and discomfited—that she lost all vital hold over herself,
and could only save herself from open confusion
by this air of wooden hardness—this appearance
of icy insensibility.

'Only a little cuss,' thought Anthony in his
adopted vernacular.

Only a cuss, but how pretty ! And where
lives the man for whom a woman's beauty does
not count as a moral grace excusing any amount
of cussedness ?

He shook hands with her as warmly as good
breeding allowed. He would have made his

hand-press warmer had he dared.   Then he said in the tone of one making a discovery :

'Why! you have grown right tall—that's a fact!'

'Yes, I suppose I am taller than when you saw me last,' said Anne, not knowing whether to most dislike the American intonation of that rich voice, or most admire the personality of the handsome speaker.

'She was only a tiny mite when you went away—just a baby,' said Mrs. Aspline, as her contribution to the inventory of reminiscences.

'Yes, just a baby,' said Anthony, still holding Anne's hands and looking into her pretty face with his searching eyes, a little deep set in the orbit and overshadowed by the straight, keen brows above. 'Why! you were just a ball in my arms. I remember how I used to toss you about!—" up to the skies and down again "—as you used to say. And how you used to kick and scream, and pretend you didn't like it, and then ask for more. Funny little thing you were! But you were a cunning little thing, too ; and now you are a young lady.'

Anne put on a dignified little look and air. It seemed somehow to rasp the fine edge of her modesties to remind her of these inconsiderate times. If her horizon, her latitude, her outlook had changed, her identity remained the same, and there had been no solution of continuity in the essential I. She was still the same actual creature as the humanized puff-ball who had been tossed up in the air by those two large hands which held her own, and grasped them with such a fervent pressure—who had been carried in those strong arms and set as a little queen on her throne on those broad shoulders— and who had been even carried pig-a-back, and kissed by those now bearded lips scores of times past counting.

'I do not remember,' she said coldly.

'I do,' said Anthony dryly.

He dropped her hands, and Anne no longer felt as if his eyes looked straight into her heart.

'Why did you not give us word of your arrival?' asked Mrs. Aspline, hospitably reproachful. 'I would have sent to the station to meet you.'

'It was not worth while,' returned Anthony.

His humaner impulses had received a check, and he had in a manner to make a fresh start. Anne's coldness had chilled him, and he did not quite see which way to take.

'It would have been pleasanter,' Mrs. Aspline insisted.

'I found a buggy,' he returned.

'That horrid fly with a broken-kneed horse !' said Anne, with a smile that was intended to neutralize the flavour of her slightly acidulated prudery.

'They mostly are in this old country,' said Anthony with a very pronounced drawl; and again Anne hated him for his voice. But how handsome he was ! How well he bore himself ! like a king for patent dignity and that superb air of self-respect which is as indescribable as an aroma but as visible as light. That subtle something belonging to all Americans who have led the adventurous life of the West—that consciousness of personal value which yet is not vanity—made itself as clear to her as her acidulated prudery had been to him, and put her in the wrong with herself. This was certainly not the man she had expected ; and it takes time to re-adjust a mental lens.

'Why, Anthony !' cried Mrs. Aspline, startled into familiarity ; 'our English horses are superior to any in the world !'

'Fact ?' queried Anthony. 'I reckon one of our mustangs would give the pick of your old three legs as many points as you asked for, and beat you at a hand-gallop after. Have you a Maud S. in any of your stables ? And which of your old weeds would carry the Yosemite stage or climb up the Rocky mountains ? No, Mrs. Aspline, America takes the shine out of you for horseflesh just as for most else. So I tell you.'

'Why, you have come back more an American than an Englishman,' cried Anne, with quite a nice little smile.

'You bet !' said Anthony briefly ; and mother and daughter exchanged glances, which Anthony smiled internally to see.

'I will fool them to the top of their bent,' he said to himself ; 'and if they see my game they are 'cuter than they look.'

But now the scene shifted altogether, and the ordinary routine of hospitality had to be gone through—the room assigned, the luggage—that one black shiny valise—taken up, and the domestic programme arranged so as to include Anthony Harford as a guest for as many days as he would care to stay, or until the terms of the trusteeship should be satisfactorily settled.

'I wish she were franker, with more go in her, more substance,' thought Anthony, as he dressed for dinner and took more than ordinary pains with himself.

'What a pity he is so Americanized! He is not like an English gentleman,' thought Anne, as she sat, her hands folded in her lap and her opaque, white, square-shaped nails horribly conspicuous, while the maid arranged her hair, put in her earrings, and dressed her as if she had been a doll or a child. 'But he is very handsome,' she thought again; 'and perhaps that bad manner will wear off in time. At any rate he is our trustee, and I am bound to make the best of him.'

But when they met, a curious coldness had

set in between them ; and Anne's charitable impulse of mild belief, like Anthony's more powerful solvent of admiration, could do nothing against the strange influence which had sent their feelings down to zero—like cream between the hasp and hinges of a refrigerator.

CHAPTER III.

UNDER THE MICROSCOPE.

THE days passed, as these days of meeting between old friends long separated always do pass, in noting the changes wrought by time, and feeling for the ground still left common. Each topic of conversation was as a landmark setting out the way and indicating the country—and these topics were inexhaustible. But it was chiefly Mrs. Aspline who talked. Anne was merely the chorus, annotating rather than amplifying; while Anthony did little more than reply, with a notable paucity of words and as notable directness to the point. Sometimes he seemed to go out of his way to offend their patriotic principles or their social prejudices by the things he said and by the manner in which he said them. He held the largest number of the gods dear to British respectability as so many battered old wooden idols, good for furnace-fires, but for little else; and his thorns crackled under various sacred pots with a concentrated scorn decidedly unpleasing. His central point was the passionless stoicism of an Indian. He would not praise and he was never angry. He could not be stirred to any kind of enthusiasm nor to any kind of righteous indignation. Had he been Red Shirt or Sitting Bull himself, he could not have been more chary of encomium on things specially Britannic. He owned up, however, as he phrased it, to the beauty of the gentlemen's parks and the smartness of the Horse Guards on parade. Almost all else was inferior to American parallels, and poor one-horse affairs generally. He nearly caused Mrs. Aspline to topple off her chair in an apoplectic fit by his strictures on the House of Lords, primogeniture, the Three Estates, and an Established Church claiming to be National in the face of all the other sects; and he pro-

duced a silence like that of death, when, to cap
his audacious idea of a great English-speaking
federation, he said that he would give the old
country fifty years, and then she would be on
her knees to the States begging to be incorporated in the Union. And when Anthony said
this, Mrs. Aspline, who had the passionate
patriotism of one who knows no other country
but her own, and who, therefore, despises all
foreign nations as inferior and comparatively
barbarous, forgot that he had ever been a
favourite with her when a boy, and Anne no
longer thought him handsome.

All the same, he showed no warmth, even
when most audacious. His lines were broad
and his words uncompromising; but he was
philosophically critical rather than passionately
antagonistic. And he was at the same time
curiously reserved. He was like one of those
huge oil-jars from which trickles the golden
fluid drop by drop—samples only of the bulk
within, but not that bulk itself. It was pro-
voking to feel that he showed so little of himself when he spoke, and was so much a mere

medium of thoughts in the general air. Why did he dribble out these mere samples of opinion instead of pouring forth himself in a generous flood that would amuse them to hear and give them something tangible to hold? They would have liked it better had he launched out into vehement denunciations instead of simply ripping up their sacred oriflammes into so many fluttering rags. Anne was as little given to hysterics as was her mother; but she, like that mother, felt the want of outflow in their new friend with olden memories, and thought him horribly cold and 'shut up.' Yet he had something in his eyes and face that was by no means cold or restricted; and though they were so often irritated with him, they were forced to respect him even when most annoyed, and to acknowledge his superiority. Deferential and full of thought for them as he was. he was yet their master; and they felt it.

To Anne this sense of power, of superiority, was a new sensation which had both its pleasure and its discomfort. This old friend with a new face seemed to her almost the only real man she had ever seen—as different from the 'curled darlings' she had hitherto known, as shadows thrown on the screen are different from real things. What did the various young curates who had meandered this way, fresh from college and the cricket-field, know of life as such a man as Anthony Harford knew it? What was their experience of 'sets' and 'dons,' compared to his of gamblers and miners, cowboys and prospectors? What learning got out of musty old tomes equalled this studied from the living page of nature and humanity? Was familiarity with the Councils and the Fathers—ability to 'find their way about patristic literature'—on a par with a man's power of finding his way over a pathless prairie, or through a tangled forest, by that sixth sense, that sublimated faculty of perception, which makes him master of things and lord of himself? Was Charlie Osborne's artistic perception of form and colour equal to this, the very highest reach to which observation can go? Was Lord Eustace Inchbold's soldiering at the Horse Guards to be spoken of in the same breath as this other's deadly encounters with bushrangers and Indians, whose treachery he divined, and, divining, frustrated? Was even Lord Royne's Indian experiences equal to Anthony's, Mexican or Texan? Was grouse-shooting or deer-stalking equal to tracking a grizzly to his own home and meeting him face to face and foot to foot in a struggle for life or death, where only a man of heroic strength and courage could win? All that Anne had ever read of adventures in any country—India, Africa, America, Canada, indifferently—trotted through her head in rapid succession; and Anthony was credited with as much prowess of a varied kind as would have set up a dozen Sir Guys or as many Cids. She was never tired of her dreams, looking at him from between her half-closed lids, and moving him over the chess-board of her fancy into all the squares that man could fill.

What Anthony thought of his fair friends and hostesses was his own secret only. Outwardly, he was quietly kind, and chivalrous as well, with a certain superficial and unobtrusive familiarity—or rather absence of formality—that had nothing in it personal, nothing dangerous. He treated Anne like a reasonable being, and neither flattered her nor made love to her. He talked to her as he talked to her mother—on the same subjects, never touching even the outside fringes of undesirable topics. He never made eyes at her; never said anything in a softer voice for no one else to hear; nor used phrases capable of bearing a second meaning. In all this he was as straight —and as uninteresting—as a die. He criticized her freely, and he laughed at her in a good-humoured, but always rather earnest, manner. He expressed perhaps more surprise than con-demnation at her indolence, her frivolous tastes, her restricted reading, her ignorance of history and geography, and the like. But his surprise was in reality condemnation. And when Anne fished for praise, as she often did, he put the line aside and refused to examine the bait.

She could do nothing with him. She had to acknowledge that to herself—that inner self to whom we never lie. Try as she would, he evaded her; and often she did not know whether to cry for mortification or to hate him for revenge; and sometimes she did both together.

All this time she felt and knew that he was watching her as keenly as the traditional cat watches the traditional mouse. She knew that he was studying her character to its depths; probing and plumbing, and saying nothing of what he dredged up. For she was perverse, like most girls, and took a wilful pleasure in making white appear black and a square look like a round, thinking that she misled him, and thus had the credit due to superior craft—and not seeing that this, too, was gauged and seen through.

If only he would have spoken and been confidential—though confidential to blame—she would have been more content. As things were, she knew that she was under a microscope; and she did not like it. She would have liked it less had she known that Anthony Harford had come in the mood which makes a marrying man—that mood which looks for causes of content and admiration rather than the reverse—and that, had she fed his nascent fire with but a sprinkling of brushwood, and not deadened it down with ashes, the whole run of his thoughts and his estimate of her would have been different. He would not have criticized so much and he would have admired more. For minds have facets which reflect according to the angle; and tender growths of feeling are killed by coldness as flowers in the garden when the frost comes. That microscope, so unsparingly applied, showed cells and fibres of which Anthony did not approve; and what might have been blind acceptance was now cold vivisection.

We all know how in a country place small events swell into importance, like those black crows of immortal memory. The fact of Anthony Harford's arrival at Hindfleet went the round of the restricted society at Kingshouse like the tearing of a piece of paper in the Ear of Dionysius. Report exaggerated and multiplied the most trivial circumstances, till a hundred artificial buds burgeoned on the original stem; and Anthony's fortune, adventures, intentions, and conditions generally, were made by fancy as different from what they were in fact as is the Hindu's sleight-of-hand, which produces wild beasts out of an empty tent, and plucks a ripe mango from a dead stick. But rumour turned her magnifying-glass chiefly on his fortune. That Thrift was a fine property as well as a pretty place every one knew; but the rent as settled by the assessor of taxes was one thing, and Anthony's private pile made in America was another. How that private pile had been made was the great Proteus of conjecture, which changed its shape in each mouth whence it issued. By gambling, said some; by mining, said others—he, Anthony Harford, the English gentleman, working like and with those ruffians spoken of by Bret Harte; by 'striking ile;' by shoddy; by slave-dealing; by political corruption; by a ring in cotton, railroads, stocks —what not. In any case, there it was; and how heavy it lay on its owner's conscience and whence it had sprung—in what slough of sin and crime its roots were planted—all these were his affair and no other person's. The one thing certain was, that pile made the income of the owner of Thrift of more value than a Scotch duke's, and worthy the consideration of a German princess.

Naturally the Asplines were 'in society' in Kingshouse; but they were not among the more cherished members. They were received, as of course, in this plutocratic age, but no one made much account of them—no one forged with them such strong links of friendship, for instance, as those which bound Lady Elizabeth and Estelle. They were slightly in a false position —social coffins of Mahomet, suspended between two terms and belonging to neither. They were above the need of such patronage and instruction as Caleb Stagg required to make him in any way passible, and they were just a line below the high-water mark of even a country place. Hence, though admitted they were not incorporated, and were only seen at the more generalized functions, whence to have been shut out would have been to be ' cut.'

Neither regretted this slender holding on to society. Mrs. Aspline was a shrewd woman, without illusions and remarkable for common sense. For her own part, she valued more her public reputation in the place than any amount of private friendship; and cared rather to be respected for her generosities than liked for herself. She was always a little shaky in her social grammar, and she knew that she was. But people could not laugh at her subscriptions, though they might at some of her nouns and adverbs. And the subscriptions made the more solid basis of the two. As for Anne, she was too indolent to desire even pleasure. She had that desperate lack in the young of want of earnestness. She was not religious, nor artistic, nor enthusiastic about anything whatsoever. She was nothing but self-indulgent in an inoffensive kind of way, leading to sleep, not sin. She was too dreamy to care for realities. Her imaginary dramas stood her in stead of action, and she preferred her own world, self-created, to that made by others. So things had ever been, 'nemo contradicente;' but now the ball had got an extra twist, and the advent of Anthony Harford had given all a different complexion. Such personalities as his do not grow like blackberries in a place like Kingshouse; and society was sore put to it how to do sufficient honour to the new-comer without demonstrating too plainly to poor Cookey that she was only the occasion and not the circumstance—an inseparable accident, but in no wise integral. Specially was Mrs. Clanricarde put to it—she who had held aloof from the Asplines with rather venomous renunciation, seeing in Anne a formidable rival to Estelle—money-bags beating beauty in the matrimonial market, and birth coming nowhere. But now, how gladly she would have rubbed out those past years on the slate of time and have made friends with one who had such a friend as this fabulously wealthy Anthony Harford! But the slate of time is a stubborn record-keeper, and only itself can efface what is written there. And Mrs. Aspline had keen eyes and a good memory. Yet she, too, was sorry she could not flourish a better social roll-call before the eyes of her guests. The winter a little helped her. ' In the country,' she said more than once, 'so little was done in the winter-time. In the summer there were garden-parties and all that, but in winter people did not care to come out.'

And Anthony, who had been so long living

out of the run of social entertainments as to have lost all taste for them and almost all remembrance, accepted her excuses as valid, and was by no means disturbed by the paucity of visitors or events.

Nevertheless, something must be done for her own credit. So Mrs. Aspline took heart of grace, and, a little abashed by her own boldness, issued invitations for a dinner party to meet Mr. Harford of Thrift. Her invitations were only to the earl and countess, Lady Elizabeth, Mr. and Mrs. Stewart, and Mr. Medlicott, the curate—a young man with a fascinating moustache like a dandy layman's and the bearing of a well-drilled officer, who wore no signs of his calling in his attire but went out to dinner in the studs, tie and swallow-tail coat of an ordinary gentleman in ordinary evening dress. Which did not prevent the queerest mixture of High Church doctrines with Broad Church practice to be found in any pulpit or any drawing-room. Accordingly, the notes were sent, and in due course the answers were received. All accepted save Lady Kingshouse; for which Mrs. Aspline was duly grateful.

It made her party more manageable as well as more evenly balanced; and it took off both a dead weight and an embarrassment. Quiet in manner and restricted in intellectual activity as Lady Kingshouse was, she was poor Cookey's social 'bogie.' Stupid as she undoubtedly was, she was none the less an adept, initiated into all the mysteries which make up the sum total of social superiority. She was one of the 'porphyrogeniti' whose dye the enriched servant could never attain—whose dye none but those born into it, indeed, ever can attain! Poor Cookey always felt as if those languid, slow-moving, slightly staring eyes were like one of her own old colanders wherein she was strained —one of her own old sieves through which she was 'passed.' She knew that every slightest infraction of the unwritten law was seen and noted; and, knowing this, her social enamel had a tendency to crack and peel off and leave the badge of the 'cordon bleu' distinctly visible. So that things were all working together for good; and the plea of indisposition on the part of my lady was gratefully received.

'We shall have a charming party, Anne,' she said to her daughter, as she flung her the decisive notes. 'I am very glad for Anthony's sake. He will see that we are respected here, when an earl can come to dinner.'

'I don't think he cares much about earls or that sort of thing,' said Anne languidly. 'He has been too long in America. He has come back such a dreadful Republican!'

'He will get over that after he has been a short time in England,' said Mrs. Aspline, sensibly enough. 'Nothing cures a man of all that wicked revolutionary nonsense so much as having property of his own. When he has got used to the possession of Thrift I don't think he will care to give it up to the socialists and dynamitards, as he pretends now he would be; and he, like every Englishman in the world, will be proud to dine with a live lord.'

'Perhaps,' said Anne. 'But then, you see, Mr. Harford is scarcely an Englishman now.'

'Oh!' said Mrs. Aspline jauntily; 'what's bred in the bone sticks to the flesh, and he can't help himself.'

'Mamma!' said Anne with plaintive remonstrance; 'how fond you are of those horrid proverbs.'

'Yes, I am, Anne; and it's a bad habit that I can't get rid of,' returned her mother penitently. 'But it's only to you, dear. I don't do much of it in company.'

'In society, of course not,' said Anne with a slight emphasis.

And just then Anthony Harford came into the room.

'Well, Anthony, I've got up my dinner-party for you,' said his hostess with a beaming face.

'Why did you give yourself this trouble?' he returned. 'We were very well as we were. Don't you think so, Miss Anne?'

'It will be pleasanter for you to see our neighbours,' she answered.

'Oh, as for that, yes. I don't object to my kind,' said Anthony laughing. 'Count or cowboy, it's all one to me so long as he goes straight.'

'Well, we have not got a count, but we have an earl for you,' said Mrs. Aspline, always beaming. 'Lord Kingshouse and his daughter, Lady Elizabeth, are coming. So it will be quite a splash affair, I can tell you.'

Anne coloured, and turned away her head.

'I am sure it will,' said Anthony good-naturedly. 'We shall have a high old time; shan't we, Miss Anne?'

'I hope you will enjoy yourself,' said Anne primly.

'And you?'

'I? I do not care for society,' she answered still primly.

'Not with a live old earl?' he asked.

'I like Lord Kingshouse and Lady Elizabeth,' she said evasively.

And Mrs. Aspline, in a pet, cried brusquely: 'Anthony Harford, if you could make my girl a little more like others—brisker and with more go in her—I'd thank you.'

'It's worth trying,' drawled Anthony coldly. Then seeing her face flame with vexation, he added with marked kindness: 'but she'll do very well as she is, Mrs. Aspline. Girls are best not all alike.'

'She might be more like others, and yet she'd be unlike enough,' said Mrs. Aspline as her parting shot, vexed beyond her usual placid good temper by Anne's almost wooden indifference to the party, the live earl, Anthony Harford, and 'every mortal thing in the world,' as she sometimes said—indifferent to such a point as if nothing but an earthquake could shake her up.

This, then, was the way in which the Aspline dinner-party came about. And the Clanricardes were out of it.

CHAPTER IV.

FRESH LINKS—I.

MRS. ASPLINE'S dinner was a success. With her delicate cuisine and admirable cellar it could not possibly be a failure. For even those who insist most strenuously on the supremacy of the mind over the body, cannot deny the geniality which comes like golden sunlight over those incarnate spirits called men and women, after they have well eaten and judiciously drunk. Nor can they refuse to see how different is this second state from the first, while brains were torpid because blood was stagnant, and good-humour was absent because the digestive organs were uneasy for want of work.

To-night all the conditions necessary for enjoyment were present.   The cuisine was perfect and the cellar faultless, as has been said.   Lord Kingshouse was a charming companion when in the vein, and he was in the vein to-night. Merely to look at Lady Elizabeth was a pleasure equal to that given by a picture by Raffaele or a spray of apple-blossom.   And then their rank in lord-loving England was as the diamond in the gold setting—the social crystallization of their personal supremacy.

Mr. and Mrs. Stewart were general favourites. Born popularities, wherever they went they were liked; at Kingshouse they were loved. Mr. Medlicott was as chirpy as a bird, and more like a bridegroom in his bearing than a man consecrated to preach of sin and death.   Anthony Harford was, of course, more interesting than anyone else to a society which knew itself a little too intimately for freshness, if it had the confidence of familiarity in its stead.   Mrs. Aspline's want of thorough breeding was well concealed under her studiously quiet manner; while Anne was just what she always was—pretty, with certain defective points, languid, negative, somewhat stupid, but perfectly inoffensive if not actively charming. She was the neutral tint among the stronger colours; and as such she had her value. That, indeed, was just her place and character. She was neutral. Gently spoken of by all, she was enthusiastically loved by none; and to Mrs. Clanricarde alone was she, in any way, a bête noire. But then maternal jealousy can make a bête noire out of a seraph or a doll indifferently.

It was, however, to Anthony Harford to whom the honour of the evening really belonged. He was a new experience to Kingshouse, and for a moment distanced even the earl. The earl himself, by the way, took to him, as the phrase goes, quite as warmly as anyone else. As, by reason of his straitened means, he had to give up much of his inherited position in the gay world—even when Parliament was sitting generally managing to pair that he might thus avoid the expenses of a London season—he was not blasé with excitement on the one hand, and he was slightly bored with his life on the other. Thus he was exactly in the frame of mind which welcomes a new-comer of interesting experiences, if that new-comer be sufficiently vouched for socially; and Anthony went in and won, as he himself would have said, 'hands down.'

As if he divined his duty to his old friend Cookey, and determined to do it gallantly, Anthony took on himself the whole burden of the man's part in the house. He told his best stories in his dry American way; and he told them with that quaint simplicity which, though it does not testify to truth, destroys all appearance of braggadocio. They were chiefly stories of his own adventures, or the adventures of others which he had witnessed. They included a great deal of promiscuous shooting, and lives carried in the hand as carelessly as a boy might carry a cock-chafer. They had to do with sheriffs; vigilance committees; jails which could not hold their prisoners, and which men in belts and boots stormed either for rescue or for lynching; horse-stealers and improvised gallows; Indians, cowboys, and buffaloes; rattlesnakes and grizzlies; with oddly-framed political notes flung in at haphazard. No one in the room clearly understood what these political notes really indicated, yet, because the names were familiar, all thought they did. Had anyone been called on to define the principles involved in this platform or that—even to tabulate the distinction between a Republican and a Democrat—he would have made a fine somersault into the vague. But Anthony assumed the knowledge he would not have found had he looked for it; and his stories were none the less enjoyed because they were only imperfectly understood.

Perhaps the men a little discounted these adventures, at least in their entirety. Aggregation is a snare to many who think it no harm to concentrate on one things which have happened to many; and to exaggerate the filling in is not like creating the skeleton out of nothing. The women were not so critical. What they did not understand they took on trust, and found the exercise of faith pleasant. A handsome man always is taken on trust by the average woman, who reserves her doubt for her pretty sisters or unpersonable brothers. And the present experience went in line with all the past. To Lady Elizabeth especially was this new-comer charming. Opposites are not necessarily antagonists. Sometimes they combine and form an amalgam, like the vinegar and sugar of a sauce. In humanity they fuse, like Desdemona and Othello, Medora and the Corsair, when set in the flame of love. So that it was not contrary to reason or fact that Anthony Harford's rough experience in the Wild West seemed to the sweetest, gentlest lady in the land—even more than they had to Anne—so many deeds of heroic manliness which claimed all men's consideration and respect.

'You have gone through terrible dangers,' she said, after his grimly quiet account of how he and a grizzly had had a hand-to-hand struggle, and how only after a fearful mauling had he been the insensible conqueror of his bleeding foe.

'Well, I have had a pretty rough time here and there,' he answered ; 'but one gets used to it, as to all things.'

'I don't think one would get used to being half-killed, as you have been so often,' said Anne simply.

Mr. Medlicott laughed a little jauntily. He had only lately come to Kingshouse, and as yet did not quite know the intricacies of the place. And, as he believed that Mr. Anthony Harford's bow was somewhat of the longest, and that his arrows went a little wildly into space, and as he thought Anne Aspline sweet and knew that she was wealthy, he was not sorry to annotate her remark with this jaunty little laugh, which gave it a certain piquancy, as a roulade of incredulity voiced a little out of tune.

A strange gleam shot from Anthony's eyes. Save for that sudden flash he did not appear to have heard either the girl or the curate.

'You see in these wild places a man has to be pretty smart in all ways,' he said, addressing Lady Elizabeth. 'He has to know how to use his hands—on man and beast.' He drew his lips close when he said this, and spoke with a certain artificial emphasis. 'Life out there is not as it is in England, where your most for-midable game is a hare or a fox, and where no man takes up a sneer for fear of creating a scene. Out there we reckon ourselves pretty much equal to all things and each other; and whether it's a grizzly or a—gentleman—we know how to meet him.'

'Yes,' said Lady Elizabeth, seeing nothing behind the mere words, which in themselves were incontrovertible. And:

'Yes,' said the old earl, with more meaning because a clearer insight. 'That makes a return to the old country, in a sense, a new experience. So much has to be unlearned, as well as a few new phases of thought and feeling to be learned.'

'As what, my lord?' asked Anthony. 'The tame acceptance of impertinence, for instance?'

'Oh,' said Lord Kingshouse with a smile; 'our duelling days are over, you see. We hold it to be both more manly and more civilized to ignore small affronts, of which the disgrace recoils on the head of the offender. Civilization demands self-suppression in more ways than one; and in this among the rest.'

'I do not hold with you, sir,' said Anthony hastily. 'A man's self is superior to all conventional rules. If his honour is touched, ever

so lightly, he should know how to defend it, and
be ready with his tools.'

'And what do you make of the sixth com-
mandment?' put in Mr. Stewart, as a kind of
protest due to his cloth.

'The Decalogue has got to take care of itself,
I reckon, when men have their shooting-irons
handy, and fools provoke them to draw,' said
Anthony slowly.

'Ah, well, we have lived out of all that rough
and ready method of self-defence,' said the vicar,
good-humouredly; 'a return to it would be
clearly a retrogression—an act of atavism—
which in these days of belief in evolution would
be a sinning against light.'

'I am afraid the sin would have to be committed if the occasion came my way,' returned
Anthony; and then the ladies rose to leave the
table, and all four were about equally shocked.

Even Anne thought her Huron was really too
ferocious. And this was the general thought.
No one took his part when Mrs. Stewart broke
out in her eager way, and said it was dreadful,
and he must be brought into a better frame of

mind. Such a fine, straightforward, handsome fellow as he was, it was a thousand pities he should be so fierce and undisciplined! And 'What savages Americans must be!' she added, as her last remark; and not even Lady Elizabeth opposed a disclaimer.

When the gentlemen appeared, however, all trace of that significant little brush had gone. The earl and Anthony had evidently fallen on some points congenial to both, and were talking in cheery tones together as they came through the doorway. The unclerical-looking curate was easy, smiling, unembarrassed as usual, but he gave the Americanized Englishman a wide berth, and was evidently on what is called good behaviour. Mr. Stewart was as he always was—kind, sincere, but a little lethargic according to the estimate of modern zeal—a gentleman as well as a parson, and a scholar rather than either. But the colour of the whole thing rested with the earl and Anthony, and the friendship they seemed to have struck up each with the other.

'Then I shall see you to-morrow?' said Lord

Kingshouse, as they parted. 'You will be interested.'

'Yes, certainly, with much pleasure, sir,' returned Anthony. 'To-morrow, in the afternoon.'

'Interested in what, father?' asked Lady Elizabeth, as they were driving home.

'In my observatory,' said the earl.

'Is Mr. Harford an astronomer?' she asked again.

'As much as all educated men are,' he returned. 'He is an uncommonly nice fellow! A little too hasty, perhaps; but that is to be accounted for by the wild life he has led. Outside his being rather too free with his hands, and too apt to take offence—that fool Medlicott very nearly put his foot in it!—he seems to be a first-rate fellow, and really Mrs. Aspline might do worse than nail him on the spot for that girl of hers.'

'She is too dreamy and unpractical for such a man; at least I should think so,' said Lady Elizabeth, feeling that Anne Aspline was in no way the right kind of wife for Anthony Harford.

'He has been accustomed to so much cleverness and quickness over there in America. I should think he would find Miss Aspline rather dull if he had to live with her always. Of course, I do not know. I only think so.'

'Oh, you Delight!' laughed the earl. 'As if men did not always like their opposites! What would become of society if two flames of fire or two bales of wool married? Why, we should run into types more marked than pouter pigeons and fantails! It is only the marriage of opposites which keeps things going at all!'

Lady Elizabeth laughed too.

'That would certainly be a reason,' she answered pleasantly. 'But I should pity poor Mr. Harford.'

'And pray why, my dear?' said her father. 'I am sure the little girl is very pretty, and fairly well mannered. If she had not one or two coarse points about her she would be really charming. But the pipkin comes out here and there; though not boldly enough to spoil her.'

'She is a good girl, I am sure,' was his daughter's reply; 'but she is rather difficult to get on with. She is what people call heavy on hand, and one can get nothing out of her.'

'Love makes a capital gimlet,' said the earl. 'You never know what a woman is capable of till she falls in love, and then you find out.'

'Yes,' said his Delight, as they drove up to the door of their home.

The next day Anthony presented himself with unholy punctuality at the exact time named by Lord Kingshouse. He had said ' half-past two or thereabouts.' As the clock chimed the half-hour, Anthony rode up to the door and rang the bell with a will, the echoes sounding like the summons of a master entering on his own. His feet fell on the stairs with the same strange kind of lordly power ; and then he was ushered into the presence of my lady, busy over her embroidery as usual.

For some little time he was alone with her ; and, unconsciously to himself, he made good use of that time, charming the lady as he had already charmed her husband and daughter. She was delighted with him, as she said afterwards. He was so fresh, so full of odd anecdotes and strange experiences, so unlike anything we know at home. And yet he was a gentleman. He was really most refreshing, and she was quite glad he had come. She was almost enthusiastic, this poor, dear stagnant lady, and carried a little beyond herself, as is the way with certain elderly women when brought face to face with a new kind of man. Her life was the dullest of the three. The earl had his public duties, as well as his fields and farms and telescope to occupy him. Lady Elizabeth had many occupations, as well as youth, to the good of her account; while she had but one amusement— crewel work, of which, however, she never got tired—no more than the lotus-eaters of their afternoons. Thus, an interesting stranger was a real godsend to Lady Kingshouse, and stimulated her like so much beaded champagne.

She was on quite a friendly footing with him by the time my lord came in; and she even sacrificed herself so far as to climb the stairs which led into her husband's observatory— spurred to this unwonted exertion by her un- wonted excitement. And when Anthony showed that he knew the constellations, as well as the latest facts and theories of what is called the new astronomy, my lord was doubly gracious to a man who could at once tackle a grizzly single-handed and understand the map of the heavens.

Then said my lady :

'You must come and dine with us, Mr. Harford. I will write to Mrs. Aspline and ask her and Miss Aspline to come too. Perhaps she will be free on Tuesday next if you are?'

'Thank you, Lady Kingshouse,' said Anthony in his quiet way. 'You are very kind, but I think I must be going home before then. I have already outstayed my time.'

'Oh, no; you can stay over Tuesday,' said Lady Kingshouse with friendly persistency.

And on the earl's seconding his wife, and Lady Elizabeth smiling her—'I should think so,' when he turned to her and said : 'What do you think, Lady Elizabeth? Do you think I may stay?' —Anthony consented for his own part, and undertook to answer for Mrs. and Miss Aspline as if he had been the son of the one and the husband of the other.

'Oh, yes, they'll come,' he said. 'They've got to.'

So there it was; and this was how Anthony Harford was induced to remain at Kingshouse for these five days longer—induced to remain, apparently for a trivial pleasure, in reality for his life's gravest destiny.

It was a pleasure to everyone alike. The Asplines wanted to keep the guest who stirred up the dull waters so delightfully; and they were moreover greatly gratified by this friendly and informal invitation from the grandest people in the place. It was the finest feather as yet stuck into their social cap; and they owed it to Anthony, who thus got good and kudos all round, both directly and indirectly. He was not slow in profiting by his opportunities. He was glad to give the Asplines pleasure. Cookey was as bright as she could be, and Anne, if of the genus little cuss, was pretty—which redeemed a good deal. As for the Kingshouses, they were purely charming. More than once he said that Lady Elizabeth was 'just lovely ; just the loveliest lady he had yet seen in the old country ;'—which superlative sometimes made both Mrs. Aspline and Anne crisp their lips as if they had eaten sour lemons without sugar.

The Kingshouse trio were glad that this very original and amusing person had been induced to stay yet a few days longer. They were more frankly interested in and by him than is the wont of great folk with anything unusual. They regarded him as almost a new specimen of the race—he was so entirely out of the ordinary groove, and so singularly delightful in his own! So that never was there a more harmonious accord of feeling—never a greater consensus of satisfaction than now, when Anthony Harford, of Thrift, near Thorbergh, had agreed to stay five days longer at Hindfleet that he might dine at the Dower House with the Earl and Countess of Kingshouse.

But before the day they all met more than once, either by virtue of that chance which governs the lives of men when chance and fate are one—or Anthony went boldly to the Dower

House, which he never left without making an appointment for another meeting. At each successive interview the friendship that had sprung up between the great family and the returned wanderer increased; and Anthony congratulated himself again and again on his happy inspiration of coming personally to Hindfleet. Anne had not wrecked his heart nor set fire to the tow of his fancy. But the Kingshouse family were friends he was glad to have made—and friends whom he intended to keep.

He had a strange feeling of moral elevation when he was with Lady Elizabeth; and when her father called her 'Delight,' he echoed the word in his own heart, and thought it exactly fitting. She was a Delight—none more so! Surely the loveliest lady of his acquaintance! Each time he saw her he thought her more supreme; and each time she fulfilled more and more perfectly his ideal of woman. And there was no posing for ideal womanhood with her as with some; no consciousness of sweet sainthood; no assumption of etherealized superiority. She was as simple as if she had been a peasant girl, and no more knew that she was like some dear angel from heaven than the south wind knows that it brings the sweet breath of flowers. That was just the beauty of it, Anthony used to think. She did not know—but he did.

CHAPTER V.

FRESH LINKS—II.

ALL who know the manner of American men and women know its curious mixture of familiarity and respect, and how its flirtatious admiration is without personal liberties of a doubtful kind. But though the unspoken mot d'ordre seems to be 'hands off!' the manner is familiar in tone and flirtatious in spirit. It has also that misleading air of specialization, of individualism, which makes it appear as if each woman were the only She, and the one in present evidence the queen of the whole sex.

No one had this manner more strongly pronounced than Anthony Harford. Excepting that it was alike to all, it was love-making to each; but to Lady Elizabeth this manner of special and peculiar devotion was more marked than to anyone else. For he did, as we know, admire her intensely. The stirred fancies of the time and the social necessities of his position which had brought him to the marrying mood, made him infinitely susceptible to the charms of such a noble creature as this dear Delight. She was so different from pretty, prim, pin-cushiony Anne, whose dear little brains were like so much delicately-tinted wool — very delicate, very charming in their own way, but only wool at the best! But this splendid specimen of English blood and breeding, this noble creature who recalled the ideal woman of chivalry, was of another pattern altogether. And Anthony was never weary of intoning her praises secretly to himself, nor of showing her openly how much he admired her. And though he did not plainly ask himself: 'Shall I?' still he let himself drift down the pleasant current of emotion and event, with the feeling of one 'seeing what would come of it.' And he took care to let Lady Elizabeth understand his mood, and trace the course of the current whereon he was drifting.

Anthony not only delicately flattered and covertly courted Lady Elizabeth, he also made her laugh, and brightened her into a state of active enjoyment, rare indeed for her to know. His stories of b'ars and 'coons and snakes, of Redskins, cow-boys, and horse-thieves, of the ranches, the prairies, the mountains and the mining-camps, were that compound of humour and seriousness which by turns touches all the feelings. Pity, horror, the appreciation of fun and the pathos of heroism—all these were struck by his skilful hand till he had touched every chord of his fair listener's heart. His quaint American accent, which he exaggerated when occasion demanded, gave additional point to his jokes and a deeper colour to his anecdotes; and his strange objurgations, which were so different from the coarser English oaths, and therefore carried with them none of their vulgarity, passed unchecked even by the sweet lady to whom swearing was specially abhorrent. He spent long hours at the Dower House,

and he went there at all times in the day; but
his mornings were chiefly passed in Lady Elizabeth's special little work-room, where he amused
himself and her by talk—or now lectured her on
her perspective, and now put in an untrained
bass to her well-taught soprano. Sometimes he
read to her; and when he declaimed those
rough Californian stories he made the poems
alive with the suppressed passion or quaint
rollick, the checked tears or the stifled laughter
which he threw into the lines.

It was all new to Lady Elizabeth, and she
enjoyed it as one enjoys a fresh breeze suddenly
blowing across a windless sky. If for many
reasons—chiefly those of outside activities and
inner content—life was not quite so dull to her
as to many others at Kingshouse, it was the
reverse of exciting; and she welcomed this
happy diversion as young people do when they
are unexpectedly taken out of circumstances
wherein they are consciously or unconsciously
bored. It was the happiest week she had ever
known. It was a week that seemed as if it had
been stolen out of the summer, and had no-

thing to do with the bleak winter in which it was set.

Yet it was not all amusement, nor all dramatic interest. Underneath the pure pleasure which Anthony Harford so largely brought was the higher sense of his manly qualities and the fine political enthusiasms which his own evoked. Essentially a Liberal, he was not a faddest. He was too broad for that, and had too much knowledge of the complexity of human nature. His great desire was to see the sun of England without a cloud in the political sky, and to know that her power was ever more firmly established. But he was an iconoclast, though a patriot; and his Liberalism stretched out into regions where that of the normal 'gentleman Radical' stops short. Broad as it was, it gained on the woman where religion made her democratic in practice for all that her abstract principles were patrician. For if she accorded so much to him when he spoke of England's true mission in the world, and how such and such virile qualities were needed for politics of the best kind, could she withstand him when he laughed at caste in favour of the individual, and classed dignities and titles with tinsel and theatrical wardrobes? When he said to her: 'You are all just in a coil of worn-out old prejudices here in England, and do not know that you are worshipping dead gods. You want the old notions to be readjusted to meet new ways'—could she refuse her assent and declare that things were perfect as they were, and needed no change at all?

He brought the sense of a freer and stronger life than any she had known before; and she supposed he understood things as she did not. Still, it took her some time to digest the new doctrine. How England's best glory was to come through the destruction of the House of Lords, the abolition of primogeniture, the nationalization of the land, and the voluntary laying down by their wearers of all stars and garters and coronets and titles, was a puzzle she did not attempt to solve. In truth, it looked more like chaos than a puzzle ; and she said so. Still, Mr. Harford said this was the only way in which England could retain—no, not retain; he corrected himself, and substituted regain—the only way in which she could regain her leading position in the race of nations. If she voluntarily tied her hands and clogged her feet with a lot of wretched stuff which the most sensible part of mankind had thrown away, she must expect to be passed; for, in spite of the old saying, the battle is to the strong and the race to the swift. And passed she would be to a dead certainty. The whole of the civilized world was pretty well up to her by now, he said; and Cousin Jonathan had forged ahead. She had made her start in former times by being the freest and most lightly held of all. While Europe still groaned under the fetters of the feudal system, she had recognized the rights of free citizenship. But she had clung too long to the rags and remnants, and she did not fitly understand tendencies. Now it was time for her to free herself from those old traditions which were fettering her, and make herself able to grow and expand according to the law of nature.

'But the aristocracy—the landed proprietors—

have done so much good! They have looked after the poor, kept society together, and been such good examples!' said Lady Elizabeth, in her high-hearted but yet so sweet and gentle way.

'They have made Lady Elizabeth Inchbold,' said Anthony quite gravely. 'That is about the best thing they have done. For that we can forgive them a few slips, like—— But I will not mention names. They may be friends of yours.'

'You mean that for kindness; but I do not think we know any reprobates,' she answered with a smile.

'Glad of it. Such as you should not. When a system has culminated—focussed itself into its best, that best should be clear of evil contact.'

Anthony spoke with a certain tender feeling underlying his artificial gravity that gave infinite charm to his words.

Lady Elizabeth laughed off the compliment with some embarrassment, and the blood came into her face.

'That is very prettily put—very charming flattery,' she said, leaning over her work-table; 'but I will take it seriously—I mean generally—and put myself out of the question. You mean the system—the peerage—has made a nobler race of men and women than the mere ordinary people. Can you say anything better? If our aristocracy has done this it has done the best it could for the country.'

'I did not say that it has given the world a nobler race,' said Anthony, quite quietly. 'I said it has made you. That is another matter altogether.'

'You flatter admirably, but you slip by the question,' said Lady Elizabeth, more and more embarrassed. 'This is not what we were talking of.'

'It is what I am thinking of,' said Anthony.

'Then between England and America, you like America best?' she asked, with curious inconsequence and strange discomfort.

His flattery was pleasant to her—was she not a woman?—but it had its element of pain too.

She did not quite know how to take it—whether as true or as a pleasant joke.

'For some things, yes. At present, I like best where I am,' said Anthony; 'in Lady Elizabeth Inchbold's little room, talking politics which she does not agree with, and fixing her palette for her next picture of "Saul and Samuel."'

'Unfixing it, you mean,' she said laughing. 'You are making it into an awful mess.'

'Satan's work, not mine. The idle hands, you know!'

'Not a pleasant association,' she returned.

'Oh, the old cuss is not so black as he is painted,' said Anthony carelessly. 'We have made far too big a scare of him. "Cloven hoof —graminivorous," as Cuvier said. We have no need to be so desperately afraid of him!'

'Oh!' said Lady Elizabeth, a little shocked and scandalized.

Like many good people who move in the ordained groove, she considered the subject too solemn to be joked about. Satan is a biblical character, she thought, and one doesn't make fun of the Bible. Anthony saw her reasoning as clearly as if it had been printed in black on white before him, and threw the conversation with a sudden jerk on to some lately-discovered fossils which had explained the mystery of the pineal gland by the third eye of the archaic lizard. And Lady Elizabeth forgave his inverted profanity for the sake of the gentleness and kindness and consideration and chivalry— and a hundred other good qualities—which made him leave the track that pained her for one which had no sharp rocks nor ledges. But this was essentially Anthony Harford's way. He was chivalrous kindness in person to women, and thought no self-suppression hard which pleased them; especially was none hard which should please Lady Elizabeth Inchbold. On which they mended that little fracture, and Lady Elizabeth thought with more clearness than ever: 'What a charming man he is; how unlike the generality of people!'—And Anthony thought, also, with more clearness than ever: 'The loveliest lady in England, bar none; just the very loveliest!'

As narrow-minded people are almost always jealous, and as Mrs. Aspline, good soul, for all her fine qualities of hospitality and sound sense, was especially narrow-minded, it was but natural that she and Anne should be a little ruffled at this pronounced preference of their guest for another house than their own. Still, they forebore to make their displeasure too evident; for had they not profited by Anthony's sudden intimacy with the Kingshouses? And might they not hope to gather still more of that coveted social wealth—the 'recognition of the best people as on terms of equality?' And if they did, it would be to Anthony that they would owe it; hence to him that they must be grateful. But it is so impossible for some tempers to keep back jibes and hints when oppressed with uncomfortable thoughts! During these intervening days Mrs. Aspline permitted herself to say more than once: 'Well, Anthony, and how are things going between you and Lady Elizabeth?' accompanying her query with a meaning laugh, which was as the feather to the arrow.

'They are going slick,' said Anthony with

a nasal drawl; 'slick as greased lightning!'

'My dear boy!' cried his hostess with a little shudder. 'When you put on that horrid Yankee accent you are really dreadful!'

'I think you do it to tease us,' said Anne, hitting the bull's-eye right in the centre.

Anthony lifted up his eyebrows.

'What in thunder do you mean?' he asked, with perfect gravity. 'What dog-gonned accent are you raring at?'

'Oh!' said Anne, covering her ears with her hands; 'you are really too dreadful, Mr. Harford!'

He laughed, and took both her hands in his. He did not like to see the vexation on her face.

'Why!' he said in a perfectly pure accent; 'what a dear little goose you are! You never did know fun from earnest, and I suppose you never will!'

Anne pursed up her nice little mouth and withdrew her hands. Naturally a prude—by the fact that her life was passed in dreams, not realities—material contact of all kinds was intensely distasteful to her.

'And the veriest prude out!' said Anthony, with a flush that made his dark eyes glitter.

'You two are always quarrelling!' put in Mrs. Aspline with a good-natured laugh. 'I don't know how it is, I'm sure. Anne thinks the worlds of you, Anthony; as I do; but there you are, cat and dog—cat and dog—and never meet but you have a scratching match!'

'Mother!' remonstrated Anne.

'Well, make Miss Anne more conformable,' said Anthony. 'At present she is all spikes—at least to me.'

'I am sorry you do not approve of me,' said Anne coldly. 'But really I cannot alter myself even to please you.'

'No, I suppose not,' returned Anthony, strolling out of the room. In a few minutes they saw him walking at a brisk pace down the drive.

'Off to the Dower House, I bet a pound!' said Mrs. Aspline; adding viciously : 'well, if he's not going to marry Lady Elizabeth he ought to —that's all I have to say.'

'Perhaps he could not if he would,' said

Anne, who 'jalousied' what she did not want
for herself.

'Could not if he would?   A beggar like Lady
Elizabeth?' cried Mrs. Aspline.   'Just let him
ask her, that's all.   If she did not jump at him,
my name's not Anne, nor yours either!'

'I am sure I do not care which way it is,' said
Anne petulantly.

'Nor I,' said Mrs. Aspline, a little venom-
ously.

CHAPTER VI.

SPREADING THE NET.

IF Mrs. Aspline's dinner had been successful, so was that at the Dower House. Larger and more inclusive, it took in all the former guests and some half-a-dozen more; among whom were Mr. and Mrs. Clanricarde. Estelle would not go. She had been asked of course, but in her self-elected state of quasi-widowhood she had preferred the solitude of home, where she might think of her distant and ever-adored Charlie, and carry her renunciation as so much sacrifice to the memory of their interrupted love. And as Mrs. Clanricarde was only cruel when the 'sacra fames' was gnawing too fiercely at her vitals, she let her daughter indulge her somewhat wayward humour, and forego the dinner which perhaps, the mother reasoned, a girl could not be expected to enjoy.   Had it been a dance she might have insisted ; but a dinner to a girl who prefers bread and butter to anything else, and calls 'à la soubise' onion sauce—that was of the nature of pearls cast before swine ; and Mrs. Clanricarde disapproved of waste.

For herself, she went to the Dower House as a matter of duty.   So she said.   It was only right to cultivate neighbourly feelings, and to help the Kingshouses when they took the trouble of entertaining such people as the Asplines.   She put on an air of saintly self-sacrifice when she said this.   She was really quite touching when she put on this air.   She did it so well, and she looked so sweet and tender!   In secret, her social creed was largely coloured by the doctrine of entertaining angels unawares; and she was always glad of a shake in the social kaleidoscope.   One never knows, she used to say to herself.   Fortunes have been left to people before now on the mere chance of identity of name—on the mere chance expression of interest—on a little service rendered at a frutiful moment when the mustard-seed was ready to start into the forest-tree. And at all times to jostle against some shining unit—some gilded fragment—gives lustre, adds consideration, and may bring profit. Gold has the habit of rubbing off, and even fragments are better than nothing. She had heard—who had not?—of this rich new man who had suddenly descended as if from the skies on the Asplines—like Jove in that shower of gold which neither ancient nor modern Danaës can resist. As yet she had not seen him. She was not on visiting terms with the Asplines;—she wished now that she had been;—Anthony had not shown at church as a good citizen and sound Churchman should have done; and the weather had been too bad for walking out. Since they had put down their carriage—oh! that unlucky George!—she had been able to go about so little, and was so dependent on the weather! Hence she had been fed only by reports of their new Crœsus, and she was not sorry to see him for herself.

All the same she tried to make herself believe
that she did not give ear to rose-coloured fables,
where the Asplines were 'les bêtes parlantes.'
She was perfectly sure—at least she said so—
that this much-vaunted phœnix would turn out
to be only a jackdaw dressed in peacocks'
feathers to deceive the unwary. A clever
person, with the gift of idealization, might, with
a few judicious verbal touches, make the most
commonplace creature a type—and as heroic as
typical. Caleb Stagg himself could be painted
up into the passable imitation of a possible
person—had she not herself borne witness to this
power, when it had suited her purpose? And
if he could be idealized into anything better than
a miner's son, brushed and washed and in his
Sunday clothes, then could this friend of those
Aspline women—this shower of gold framed
like a man, and come as a second Jove from the
sky. As their friend, indeed, he could not be
worth much; and she did not believe in Lady
Elizabeth's judgment. Lady Elizabeth was a
dear creature—a very dear creature—but she
had her 'manies' like anyone else; and every

goose in her flock was a snow-white royal swan.

No; she, Mrs. Clanricarde, the wife of a ruined husband and the mother of a beautiful daughter, would see things with her own eyes before she allowed her hope to run away with her, as it had done more than once in her life before. This time she would be cautious; and she would test the ground before trusting herself to walk on it.

With the secret determination to fascinate this new-comer, whom yet she spoke of with not so much judicious reserve as prepared hostility, Mrs. Clanricarde dressed herself with more than ordinary care—and she was never negligent of her appearance. Indeed, she would have found a prison tolerable with a pier-glass and superb toilettes. To-night she made herself really beautiful; for she was one of those pretty women who know every turn and trick of adornment. Had she been Estelle herself, free-hearted, in the marriage market and anxious for a settlement, she could not have been more solicitous to look well—more particular in her methods. And the result justified the means. She looked superb; and she knew it. She had that indescribable ‘chic,’—that look of foreign distinction, which no daughter of Albion can imitate. She was like some old picture of Watteau—the French marquise of tradition translated into modern life; and that skilfully applied hare's-foot, with that one artful little patch, completed the charm.

‘How handsome you look to-night, Louise!’ said that unlucky George, seeking to propitiate his tart-tempered goddess, as well as sincerely stirred to unwonted admiration.

He laid his hand on her white, plump arm with a caressing, half-timid touch.

‘It is a wonder that I have any looks at all after your conduct,’ was her cold reply, drawing away her arm as if some creeping thing had crawled over it.

And her facile, foolish, good-natured husband, with his restless eyes and fatuous smile, sank into silence and calculated the gains that would come from that last investment in a newly-discovered diamond-mine. She was long past that state of mind when his compliments could enliven her, or his caresses give her pleasure. The utmost limits to which her philosophy could reach was to bear with him in silence—which was not in patience.

At dinner Mrs. Clanricarde was seated next to Anthony Harford; and on her, as on every-one, his wonderful manner of mingled naïveté, reserve and dignity made the sharp impression of a new experience. That odd combination of the Wild West 'scout' with the English gentle-man gave him a flavour as of a cultivated wild fruit. He was as delightful as the Huron, and Mrs. Clanricarde did what she could to improve her chance. Though not her assigned cavalier—this was Mr. Stewart, whom she knew by heart—she talked to Anthony Harford as some women do talk at dinner to the wrong man, to the exclusion of their own partner. And he, though seated next to Lady Kingshouse, was not unwilling to divide himself between the two. The vivacity of this striking-looking woman, with her dark, bright eyes, and prema-turely white hair dressed á la Pompadour,

amused and interested him. She was brighter
than the general run of Englishwomen, he
thought; bright enough for a Bostonian, had
her good angel willed her that supremacy; and
so far as she went she was unique. She was a
decided improvement on that good, fat, gener-
ous-handed Cookey, if not quite up to the Kingshouse mark. They, indeed, were supreme, and
his admiration for them was a veritable enthusiasm. They were so nobly simple in their
comparative poverty—so truly the old ideal of
English aristocracy. The countess was 'grande
dame' even over her embroidery; and Lady
Elizabeth was the very flower of humanity—the
very essence of spiritual beauty. Anne Aspline
had by now fallen into complete insignificance.
She had drifted to the rear in the social
phalanx which was headed by this one delightful figure—this Aslauga, with her golden tresses
—this Iseult, with her slender throat and gentle
smile. He did not know, but he half believed
that he was in love with Lady Elizabeth. He
was not sure, for he felt for her differently from
what he had ever felt for any woman in his life

before; and he was not quite able to analyze his own sensations. Nor did he know her mind. She was sweet and friendly and gracious as a wingless angel might be. But how about the woman? He had watched her these last days as keenly as he had sometimes looked for the trail of an Indian or for the smoke of a sheltering cabin. He fancied that her cheeks had taken a deeper colour when he came upon her suddenly in the lane—that her eyes looked both brighter and softer when they met his— that, when he entered the room this evening, that inner kind of smile which tells of secret pleasure had come over her face like so much sunlight. He fancied all this—he did not know. The reserve of a modest English girl makes divination difficult. Anthony was no fop, and he was afraid to think that these shadowy signs meant more than so many accidents with which he had really no vital connection. He was a little at sea all through, and so was forced to let things drift: conscious only that this lovely-minded girl spoke to his higher nature as no woman yet had done, and made him feel as if he must be his best self when in her presence. But how she regarded him—that was her secret; and he could not fathom it; at least not yet.

Nevertheless, though these thoughts hung about him with a filmy kind of consciousness, like a mist-wreath rising from the mountain, he enjoyed Mrs. Clanricarde's vivacious talk, as she intended he should; contenting his sense of fidelity by looking across the table at Lady Elizabeth, sitting immediately opposite, and including her in the conversation whenever he had the chance. And how beautiful she looked to-night! Not with the beauty which stirs a man's senses, or mounts like strong wine to his brain, but with the beauty that calms while it inspires—that brings the glory of heaven down to the earth for sweet sustenance and illumination. Anthony thought her again and again the loveliest lady he had ever seen; and wondered, with increasing wistfulness, what she thought of him, and whether she liked him in truth and very deed—liked him below the surface and not only just on it.

Thus the dinner passed, and everyone was

amused and thought it the pleasantest ever given at the Dower House—and wished that the Kingshouses were richer, and could launch out into the same kind of entertainments as those of olden days, which had helped to impoverish them now—and in the wish scraped off some of the lustre of their pleasure by regret, and watered down their wine quite unnecessarily. But this is after the manner of men, who will look before and after whatever it costs them!

When the gentlemen came into the drawing-room, Anthony went straight to where Lady Elizabeth and Mrs. Clanricarde were sitting together, discussing Shakspere and the musical glasses with apparent interest and real flatness —Lady Elizabeth thinking of Anthony Harford with pleasure, Mrs. Clanricarde with unrest. As he joined them, what was dark to Anthony was clear as daylight to Mrs. Clanricarde, and she read in a glance what he had not spelt correctly after long looking.

'She is in love with him,' thought Estelle's mother; 'and I will conquer.'

Something stirred her as if it had been a sword drawn from its scabbard. The passion of the fight, love of intrigue, desire of conquest, all leaped up in sudden flame in her heart. Born for this kind of warfare as she was, how seldom had her talents been utilized here in this old Sleepy Hollow—this Noah's-ark kind of society! But now had come the hour—and the man; and Mrs. Clanricarde consecrated herself to the struggle as fervently as ever a young squire consecrated himself to the laws of his new knighthood.

'Will you come and see me, Mr. Harford?' she said in her blandest way. 'I have a few old Japanese curios that are very rare. Some of them indeed are unique, and were brought from Japan when the manufactures were not spoiled for the English markets, and before collecting had become a passion. I shall be glad to show them to you if you care for such things. They are fine, are they not, dear?' to Lady Elizabeth.

'Beautiful!' answered that guileless Aslauga. ' Quite worth seeing,' she added.

'Thank you. I will go with pleasure,' said Anthony.

He had not the faintest notion who Mrs. Clanricarde was, nor where she lived, but Delight would tell him, and perhaps accompany him. She was a very amusing and vivacious lady—that was all he knew and all he cared for at the present moment.

'When will you come—to-morrow?' she asked. 'How long do you stay at Hindfleet? Perhaps in any case, you had better come to-morrow.'

'Yes, I will call on you to-morrow,' he answered. 'I am not staying many days longer. I have out-stayed my time as it is.'

'I am sure you will admire my curios,' she repeated.

'I am coming for you, not for your old relics,' he said bluntly.

And Mrs. Clanricarde's heart gave a throb like a girl's. If this stranger were so easily charmed with her, what would he be with Estelle? And what a splendid-looking creature he was!—really a conqueror among heroes! How far had he gone with Lady Elizabeth? Not very far, she thought. She was as astute as any human being could be, not to have more than the normal senses, and she did not see any indications of an express understanding between them. She thought that he was fishing and she was nibbling; but, what of that! Her drag-net would take the ground, and all else would be of no avail. So they parted, and it was agreed that next day Anthony should go to Les Saules to call on Mrs. Clanricarde, and see her old Japanese curios, bought before the manufacture of porcelain, enamel and lacquer had been ruined to suit the debased taste of the red-haired, ' foreign devils.'

' Oh !' said Mrs. Aspline, with the briskness of a sour ferment, when he told her of his engagement; ' that's in the wind, is it ?'

' What is in what wind ?' he asked.

' Well, you have fallen into the hands of the Philistines, that's all,' she answered. ' This Mrs. Clanricarde is the most manœuvring woman in Kingshouse. She is like a spider with flies. You are done for, Anthony, if you do not see through her.'

He laughed.

'I am not afraid of her,' he said lightly.

'It would be better if you were,' said Mrs. Aspline sharply. 'Pride goes before a fall, Anthony, and you are not the first man who has fallen into a trap.'

'Don't see the trap,' he returned.

'And I do,' said Cookey with a certain viciousness by no means usual to her.

'And then she is so proud,' said Anne languidly; 'and what of, I should like to know? They are ruined, and everyone expects to hear of their being sold up—any day. Why should they be proud?'

'Then you, too, don't like them?' asked Anthony,

'I? Like them?' she answered quite quietly. 'I seldom dislike any one, do I, mother? But if there is one person in the world that I hate it is Mrs. Clanricarde. I wish she was dead!'

Anthony looked at her in amazement.

'What queer cusses women are,' he thought to himself.

What was the meaning of all this? What

corn of poor, fat, good-natured Cookey's had this quasi-Bostonian trodden on? Where had sleepy, stupid, unpractical little Anne been pinched? He remembered how these ladies had exchanged only the most glacial salutations last night. Their mutual attitude had been that of so many clothed and decorated icebergs. What tempest in a teapot had shaken these atoms into antagonism, and what was the solution of the mystery?

All that, however, was their affair. He had nothing to do with it. As a gentleman he must keep his promise to this alert French marquise-like woman; a promise which, if the Asplines had given him the map of the country in good time, he would probably not have made. But Mrs. Aspline had said nothing. She never did speak against her neighbours. She was far too clever, knowing that, for a woman of doubtful holding in her own person to be cited as a slanderer, a retailer of unsavoury stories, an utterer of ill-natured remarks, is to socially saw the branch on which she is sitting and to come headlong to the ground. Only when caught out by the sudden impact of an unpleasant surprise, did she forget her habitual caution and launch forth impolitic objurgations—as now to Anthony, with whom, however, no harm was done. He was not the man to repeat nor betray; and he would not tell it even to the reeds that she had said this special Midas had ass's ears beneath her crown. But she was vexed and annoyed, more than she could say, that he had undertaken to go to Les Saules, fearing she knew not what of loss to herself and complications all round.

CHAPTER VII.

HIS FATE.

THE next day Anthony prepared to go to Les Saules, as agreed on. Mrs. Aspline had evidently forgotten the engagement, for she proposed that her guest should drive with her and Anne to see the Fairy Howk, which was one of the 'points' of the place, and which would be so lovely to-day! There had been a two days' sharp frost, and the icicles would be now beautiful—really something worth seeing.

'You will come of course?' she said, with a flushed face and a rather quick voice.

'Where is your Howk?' asked Anthony. 'In what direction?'

'Through Kingshouse and on the Lancaster road.'

'Anywhere near Les Saules?'

'Les Saules!' Mrs. Aspline spoke in a tone of surprise. 'Oh dear no! What have we to do with Les Saules?'

'Well, I have if you have not,' he returned. 'I am going to see Mrs. Clanricarde to-day.'

'Oh!' said Mrs. Aspline crisping her lips. 'So you persist, do you?'

'Persist in keeping an appointment?' he laughed. 'Why of course I do.'

'Then you'll repent it,' said Mrs. Aspline, turning coldly away, as one who turns from a son of perdition finally abandoned to his evil ways.

It was all very inexplicable to Anthony, and he exhausted conjecture in vain. He finally came to the conclusion that the lively, half-foreign looking woman was a runaway wife, whose little slip society had agreed to condone in a half-hearted way—strict sisters, like that virtuous and astute Cookey, holding aloof, no matter who drew near. He was sorry to offend his hostess, but an engagement is an engagement; and Anthony was not the man to allow his actions to be influenced by anyone, man or woman, and woman no more than man. He would do what he had undertaken to do, and make it all right with the Asplines when he came home. He would thus sit on the two stools of tradition, and not come to the ground. He would hold with the hare and hunt with the hounds, and have the good of both runs. He would have a pleasant talk with that entertaining lady, who might almost have been a Bostonian; and he did not see what harm could come of it, nor why his old friend should 'ra'r.' He was not going to make love to her, nor carry her off 'vi et armis' from her good-looking husband with the weak chin and fatuous smile; and he could not for the life of him see any valid objection to the arrangement, turn it which way he would. Meanwhile, he would go round by the Dower House, and see that dear Delight whose presence always brought him the sense of spiritual harmony and mental rest. He had more faith in her common sense than in that of his older friend. Perhaps through her he should come to the heart of the mystery in re the Clan-ricardes and get an insight into causes hidden from him now.

But Lady Elizabeth could not help him. All she could give him was the rather bald bit of information : 'They do not like each other.'

'But why?' asked Anthony, who knew the fact and wanted the reason.

'I do not know, except that Mrs. Clanricarde did not call on the Asplines when they came,' she answered.

'But why?' he asked again.

'Mrs. Clanricarde is very proud, and has great ideas of birth and all that,' said Lady Elizabeth reluctantly.

She did not like to allude to Mrs. Aspline's industrial origin to her friend and guest.

'Because she was once a cook?' said Anthony bluntly, cutting the Gordian knot with one blow.

'Yes, I suppose so,' was the answer.

The Americanized Englishman laughed.

'Good God!' he said with that kind of mirth which has in it more gall than honey. 'As if it

signifies a red cent whether she were a cook or
not if she knows how to behave herself, and
bore a good character before and after! I
should have thought that Lady—Mrs. Clanricarde—had more sense than to stumble into
this hole. Also,' he added, looking at Lady
Elizabeth with eyes as soft as satin, 'I should
have thought that what Lady Elizabeth Inchbold patronized might pass muster with all the
world beside in Kingshouse.'

Lady Elizabeth smiled with the pretty faint
embarrassment she so often showed when with
Anthony Harford. Flattery, which from anyone
else was especially displeasing to her, from him
was delightful. Yet she never knew whether
to accept it in silence or to disclaim it as undue.
Had it come from anyone else she would have
shown that she disliked it. From Mr. Harford
it was different. He was not quite an Englishman now; and we owe more consideration to
quasi-foreigners than to our very own unadul-
terated; and he was more sensitive than most
people, and bore more uneasily with check or
rebuke. Hence she let the compliment slide;

and Anthony thought how sweet she looked when she dropped her eyes like that, and the colour mounted over her blush-rose face just enough to swear by. How sweet she was altogether! He was conscious that he was steadily drifting—not swiftly—not over rapids and cataracts with a swirl and a rush—but slowly and quietly—drifting almost lazily, like a leaf on a summer stream—to the broad still haven of assured happiness and confessed love. But he would do nothing rash. He would be sure of her mind before he showed his own. He was not the man to brook a refusal; and he had learned caution before making big bets.

'But there is nothing against either the one or the other?' he asked again. 'My old friend Mrs. Aspline, I know, always conducted herself like a lamb. Has Mrs. Clanricarde as clean a record?'

'Quite,' was the answer. 'It is only a personal feeling. Perhaps, as mothers, they are mutually jealous of their daughters.'

'Daughters? Has Mrs. Clanricarde a daughter?'

'Yes; Estelle. A very pretty girl, and a very dear one.'

Lady Elizabeth spoke warmly. She dearly loved Estelle—and she pitied her as much as she loved—which gave a certain flavour of tenderness exquisitely charming.

'Why did she not come here yesterday?' was Anthony's next query.

'She is not very well,' answered Lady Elizabeth. She did not say, 'She is broken-hearted because her lover has gone away.'

'Oh! now I see it all,' cried Anthony with sudden illumination. 'Why, of course. How dense of me not to have seen it before. Jealousy. There it is. Well! you women do beat creation for that!' he added. 'You *are* jealous among yourselves, and that's a fact! We men are nowhere compared to you.'

'I think you do pretty well, however, in that line,' was Lady Elizabeth's laughing reply; but Anthony, with emphasis, repeated his asseveration, and declared that women were the most jealous beings on earth, and beat all creation hollow, let what else would make the running.

Then he rose to leave, and holding Lady Elizabeth's hand just a moment longer than necessary, he said, looking at her again with his satiny eyes:

'But you are above that trash, I am sure! I should as soon expect lightning from a rainbow as jealousy from Lady Elizabeth!'

'I hope I should never be so poor-hearted nor mean-spirited,' was her answer, made gravely and with earnestness.

'The loveliest lady in England!' was Anthony's unspoken thought, repeated two or three times, as he went on his way to Les Saules—'just the loveliest! She has a heart as pure as crystal and a mind as bright as silver. I wonder if she could ever be brought to love me? She is worth trying for. With such a wife as that all my unrest would be over—all my fever would be quieted. I should turn then to the real country gentleman's life, and be a model landlord and a just magistrate. She would help me to be good. She is goodness herself incarnate. No man could be aught but his best self when with her; and her love would honour the proudest and add lustre to the best. If she could be brought to really love me? Does she in any degree already? Sometimes I think she does, and then—I would not like to bet on it! She is so sweet and gentle to every one—but she does not change colour so often to any one else as she does with me. I wonder!— or am I a darned fool?'

And as he thought this last phrase, he turned into the gate of Les Saules, and soon found himself in the room where Mrs. Clanricarde was alone.

She received him graciously; with just that amount of cordiality which keeps on the right side of gush and is as far from niggardliness as from excess. She said she was glad to see him, and she did not ask after his hostesses. She spoke of the pleasant dinner they had had yesterday evening, and called Lady Elizabeth a dear soul; though she greatly lamented her want of practicality—or rather, her regret was as a fringe to her admiration; for she first praised her for her goodness and then added the deprecating addenda, as one who should remark on

the rather rumpled condition of a shining
garment, and the slightly tattered state of a
phœnix's tail-feathers. The shining garment
was a fact, and the phœnix was a fact; and the
rumpled condition of the one, and the tattered
state of the other, did not lessen the essential
value of either. All the same—she lamented.

'In what way is she unpractical?' asked
Anthony, feeling as if his lance were in rest
and the bugle had sounded.

'She is too good,' returned Mrs. Clanricarde
with a soft smile. 'As if anyone can be too
good! I suppose I ought to say that we are all
too bad for her.' She said this with the nicest
little air of apology and self-accusation. She
was really a wonderfully charming woman!

'To be too good is not a very general fault,'
said Anthony, answering her smile. 'For me, I
think Lady Elizabeth just perfect.'

'She is indeed delightful,' returned Mrs.
Clanricarde. 'It is a pity she belongs to such
a family.'

'What of them?' he asked gravely.

'Do you not know?—there is madness among

them,' she answered. 'Some of them are now I believe, in a lunatic asylum. It is that which makes me regret the dear love's decided eccentricity as I do. If her family history was not darkened by this terrible scourge, she might be as odd as she liked, and one would only love her all the more, and say it was her way—and, being hers, beautiful! But now, come and look at my curios, Mr. Harford. I have really a very notable collection.'

She had, however, taken the heart out of him for the moment, and he could think of nothing but the terrible shadow on the path of his sweet friend. And for awhile Mrs. Clanricarde thought she had made a mistake, and done more harm than good by her false information. She recovered her lost ground with infinite pains, and only after a time. Her vivacity was infectious, and Anthony could not resist the contagion. He handled her queer little squat figures, and dislocated monsters with wry necks and shaven heads—pronounced them interesting and thought them hideous. He looked at her photographs of places and pictures, and thought that the ruins would be better for the builder and the figures greatly improved if put into better drawing. He criticized the early Italian artists and the Byzantine mosaics, like the rank outsider and Philistine he was; and he forgot that æstheticism was a cult as dear to its votaries as any religion ever promulgated. He made Mrs. Clanricarde think him an Orson and a boor, intellectually taken; but he made her resolve on her plan of campaign with even more and more determination. She was not sure that she should succeed, but she would make a bold stroke for it; and Lady Elizabeth must be put out of court.

Then, as Anthony, having exhausted the outside world as represented here in the drawing-room at Les Saules, was beginning to take leave, she stopped him by saying as a kind of after-thought—a kind of minor and even minimus attraction—'Oh, by the way, I must introduce you to my daughter before you go. She is upstairs, painting. She is so fond of art!—and is really not a despicable artist; at least, naturally, I think so.'

'Oh, yes! your daughter. I should like to see Miss Clanricarde,' said Anthony, who had forgotten her existence.

Mrs. Clanricarde rang the bell and asked the servant to beg Miss Clanricarde to come down. She spoke smoothly and gently, as one who speaks of a creature infinitely beloved—seeming to linger on the name with delicious tenderness. She was standing near the door, and Anthony did not hear her rapid whisper to the maid: 'Do not say that anyone is here.' He only heard the indescribable accent of affection—affection mingled with the loveliest courtesy.

'That is the way a mother should speak,' he thought to himself; and for the sake of this maternal sweetness he forgave the vivacious Frenchwoman her unwelcome news about Lady Elizabeth.

In a few minutes the door-handle turned and the door opened. Framed as in a picture—checked by the momentary surprise of finding a stranger where she expected to see only her mother—Anthony saw a tall, dark-haired girl, with soft brown eyes and a pale flower-like face, dressed in a quaintly-fashioned gown of clinging material and indeterminate colour— neither blue nor green, but between both;—a girl whose beauty was great but whose charm was greater—that subtle, nameless charm which belongs to the fated and fateful women of men's passion and destruction—the charm which Helen and Cleopatra and Mary Stuart had to their sorrow and the sorrow of those who loved them. Her eyes were worlds in which the soul was lost. Her smile was a net wherein the senses were entangled. Her dark and curling hair was like the perfumed tendrils of a dusky vine. Her lithe and graceful figure had in it the sense of melody and rhythmic harmonies in every line and every gesture. She stood there, as she might have been, the blessed damozel against the golden bar of heaven; and Anthony caught his breath as at a vision seen in the twilight. He felt as if the whole meaning of his life had suddenly been made clear—as if he had looked into a magic crystal and seen the hidden secrets of fate and the future. A fire seemed to run through his veins; and there broke out in him that wild fever which gives a man twice the power he had before. He knew that he had looked into the face of his Fate, and seen the angel who was to lead him to his bliss or his despair. All the loves and fancies of his past years shrivelled up before this wonderful revelation as the leaves of a forest when the simoom passes over them. A swift rush of thought brought the image of Lady Elizabeth before him, and it seemed to him as if she were the moon when the morning sun has risen. She passed into a kind of vaporous and lovely unsubstantiality, while here he was in the presence of the true and only one.

In the brief moment while Estelle stood there and he looked at her, he seemed to live years and to go through the experience of a lifetime. Something woke up in him that had been dormant for all his life, and he came suddenly to the possession as of another sense—to the full inheritance of his soul. Then the spell shifted— it did not break—as Estelle, letting the door fall from her hand, came slowly into the room and was formally introduced. And Anthony, who had adopted the American habit of shaking hands on an introduction, was afflicted with a sudden and to himself an incomprehensible shyness, and felt as if he dared not touch that long white graceful hand—no more than an ordinary knight dared have touched the San Graal, had he seen it.

After this he lost count of time. He could never remember how long he stayed nor how he tore himself away. He only knew that he found himself at last at Hindfleet—in his heart as it were a bird singing, a fountain playing, a garden blooming—and the dull winter evening changed to an infinite glory of great gladness —which yet was akin to tears.

CHAPTER VIII.

AT THE KINGSHOUSE ARMS.

THE position was undoubtedly awkward. Anthony Harford was the guest of Mrs. Aspline, who hated the Clanricardes, who did not visit the Asplines. What was to be done? There is a certain honour to be observed in small things as in large, and it savours of treachery and disloyalty to make a friend's house the point of departure for negotiations with his enemy.

At first, after he came back from Les Saules, and while his whole being was full of that new charm—like music still vibrating in the air— Anthony had done his best to bring about some kind of better feeling on the part of that usually good-natured Cookey—that naturally gentle, because phlegmatic, Anne. But he found them obdurate. Their pride had been wounded; their social interests had been damaged by the Frenchwoman's pronounced disdain; and feelings are like everything else—the longer they have lived the tougher and harder they become, till time does his inevitable work, when they fall into dust and nothingness under his hand.

Here, then, was the awkwardness of the position. Anthony would not leave Kingshouse just yet, and he could not stay at Hindfleet if he intended to improve his acquaintance with the Clanricardes, as he certainly would. For what else should he remain here at all? Even Lady Elizabeth, sweet as she was and delightful as he had found her—just on the brink, too, as he had been; just on the brink, looking for her face in the magic fountain—even she could not have kept him; nor could her people, nor could his present hostess. But that tall, dark-haired girl, with her fated charm —ah! that was another matter! To see her again and often—to get to know her and to prove her—to win her to himself, and wear her on his heart for all his life, as his flower of love and the jewel of his treasury—yes, for Estelle he must stay and could not go. And yet he could not stay at Hindfleet.

Wherefore, making so far a clean breast of it, he told Mrs. Aspline what was on his mind as relating to her and 'those people at Lissols,' as she called them; and how impossible he felt it to accept her hospitality while using his time in visiting a house which had shut itself against her, and which now she would not visit were it opened to her.

'I am sorry for you, Anthony,' said Mrs. Aspline, flushing a violent crimson passing into purple. 'You are not the first man that manœuvring old cat has caught, and you will not be the last. I thought you had more sense. You are old enough, I am sure.'

'Old enough to know my own mind?' said Anthony gravely. 'I hope so.'

'When you say the Clanricardes, you mean Miss,' continued Mrs. Aspline. 'I do not suppose you care much for that fool of a man who is next thing to a natural, or for Mrs. Clanricarde either, with her pride and her finery. At her age, dressing as she does to look like a picture! I have no patience with such vanity! It's not decent; and so I tell you.'

Anthony was silent. It did not come into the programme of his duty, as he conceived it, to defend Mrs. Clanricarde's millinery; but he thought again, as so often before: 'What queer cusses women are when they come to logger-heads among themselves!'

'Take our advice,' said Anne, putting on a little maternal air that was both becoming and entertaining; 'go home to Thrift, and keep out of danger. You will repent it if you stay here. We know all about these people better than you do.'

'I do not suppose there is much harm to know of them,' said Anthony, even more gravely than before.

'Well, I don't know what you call harm,' said Mrs. Aspline. 'If right and left, and Tom, Dick, and Harry's no harm, then there is none,

I suppose. But I know I would have been sorry enough if any daughter of mine had been hawked about all over the place, as Mrs. Clanricarde has hawked hers!'

Anthony's bronzed face became strangely livid as well as stern. It seemed to suddenly set like so much metal, and to become rigid like death.

'I reckon there's not much chance of hawking any girl about in such a God-forsaken old place as this,' he said with forced quietness.

'Then isn't there, just!' returned Mrs. Aspline. 'First, that Mr. Charles Osborne, who has a cough like a churchyard and not a penny-piece to bless himself with; and then that mooncalf up at Redhill yonder, that Caleb Stagg, that I declare I would not touch with the end of a mop-stick. That woman there flung her daughter at these two, and would have given her ears for either. The way she went after that young Stagg was what I call a disgrace. And all the world knows it, as well as I.'

Anthony drew his lips close together as people do when they are deeply moved, and yet wish to keep their self-command. Could he have ever liked this woman—this vulgar traducer of that exquisite vision? Mrs. Aspline took a new face and form and meaning for him. She was no longer the kind old Cookey of his boyish days—still less the improved, hospitable, almost lady-like woman of this latter time. She was a vulgar scold; and his heart sickened against her.

She saw that she had made a mistake.

'Well, there! I was wrong to put myself about like this,' she said with a forced laugh. 'You are old enough to know your own mind, as you say, Anthony; and you have seen enough of the world by now to find your own way about. And I daresay I am prejudiced against this Mrs. Clanricarde and all her kith and kin. They have not been over-civil to Anne and me, and naturally we resent being treated like dirt under their feet. But it's all right, I daresay; and you are your own master. So let us say no more about it, and I'm sorry I spoke.'

'It is as well to know all sides,' said Anthony, speaking with difficulty. 'They stoned the saints once on a time, and they keep up the practice yet.'

Mrs. Aspline flushed again as before; Anne bit her lips; but both kept silent and chewed the bitter cud with decorous resignation. It seemed little less than blasphemy to compare the Clanricardes—Estelle or her mother—to saints; but Anthony Harford was—well! he was a Harford; and the Harford mouth was hard. It would take a stronger hand than either Anne's or her mother's to rein in this runaway if he chose to go to destruction. So they felt, and on this they acted, and shut down the Pandora's box of ill-words and ill-feeling before reconciliation had taken flight with the rest. But Anthony's heart was still sick and sore, and his spirit revolted against his former flowery fetters.

'I reckon,' he said after a moment's pause, 'I shall be doing the square thing if I clear out of this and make new tracks. As I am going to see for myself what these ladies are like, and calculate to be pretty near half my time at Les Saules, it will be better for us all if I take rooms at the hotel, where I shall offend no one and be in no one's way.'

'That, of course, is as you like yourself,' said Mrs. Aspline, with the dignity of displeasure. 'You are not in our way here, Anthony, and I hope we have not shown that you were. I hope we have made you comfortable, and let you see that you were welcome. We have done our best.'

Here the poor dear woman's voice a little broke, and her eyes grew red. The rain threatened after the thunder had growled.

'You have been just as kind as ever you could be,' said Anthony. 'There's nothing to be said on that, and I'm ever so much grateful to you. But I reckon it will be squarest to clear out now, and likest to keep us good friends.'

'Very likely,' said Mrs. Aspline, curiously lachrymose and indignant at one and the same time.

'Perhaps you are right,' said Anne.

Vexed to see her mother so moved, she took a tone as hard and cold as an iron rod—as acid as so much lemon juice. For all her vague dreams, she had not dreamed herself in love with Anthony Harford. It was doubtful, indeed, if she could ever love anyone but the unsubstantial figures which her fancy projected on the screen, and which had nothing to do with life at all. Be that as it may, this handsome Huron—this mild-mannered, grave and thoughtful Corsair—remained where he was; or rather his shadow had passed into the darkness of the night, and of the substance she made no account.

'Then that is all fixed and straightened out,' said Anthony with a sense of relief.

'Certainly,' said Mrs. Aspline; and 'Certainly,' echoed Anne.

Which ended the matter and clamped the proposition into its final affirmative. So that night saw Anthony Harford installed at the 'Kingshouse Arms,' where he intended to remain for at least some weeks.

He could not go back to Thrift. How cold and gloomy and desolate the old place looked in his memory! His imagination peopled it with chill shapes of distressful meaning, and it was to him now as if he had lived in a tomb while there. He would not go back till the winter had passed and the spring had come with its verdure and its flowers—till the running of the sap in the trees stirred nature to renewed life, as the hopes and thoughts of men were stirred to passion by the red blood within their veins. It wanted sunshine to make it habitable—ah! more sunshine and of a different kind from that which flowed from summer skies to lie like a radiant veil over the earth! He knew well what it wanted. There was no uncertainty here—no tentative questions were put to his heart and consciousness. His heart and consciousness overwhelmed his judgment. He only knew what he felt, what he hoped, what he had set himself to do; and he asked nothing more than—Let me have time and a clear field. He was well as he was. This rat-haunted, ill-found little inn, smelling of old woollen and dry-rot, was as sweet as a pathway in Paradise, and this 'god-forsaken old hole' of Kingshouse was as fair as an oasis bearing palm trees and white lilies.

VOL. II.

Everyone was glad to hear that Anthony Harford had moved into the town. It was an earnest of his continued stay; and it made intercourse with him so much the freer now that he was not tied to the Asplines, for whom no one specially cared, and with whom no one wished to knit up an intimacy. It was somewhat a surprise, however; for no one knew why he stayed—and at such a very second-rate kind of place as the 'Kingshouse Arms!' To be sure the Asplines knew, but they kept their own counsel; and Mrs. Clanricarde guessed, but she, too, kept hers.

A curious little warmth spread over Lady Elizabeth's heart when she heard the news; and her fair face took the colour of her feelings. No one noted that swift and sudden flush; and to herself it bore no significance. She did just quietly wonder why her cheeks so suddenly seemed to burn, as if the fire had scorched them or the hidden sun had touched them. But that was all. It was one of those small personal matters which make no mark on the memory, because so little on the consciousness. Only it was certain that she was glad he was going to stay, and she said so. Why not?

As for Anthony, had he been there he would no longer have noticed whether the fair cheeks flushed or paled—whether the soft eyes brightened or were abashed. These signs were signs to him, no more. The saint had gone back to her shrine, and her womanhood had vanished in the smoke of the scented incense. The ideal had clothed itself once more with the glory of the unattainable and the impersonal. Aslauga's golden tresses were the rays of the eternal sun, and no longer the living hair of love. The human fancy which had for a moment disturbed that saintly purity and brought it nearer to the earth—which had touched that tender and almost solemn loveliness and brought it within the compass of a man's desire—that fancy had died before it had been fairly born; and to Anthony, as to Caleb, Lady Elizabeth was the being to worship, but Estelle was the woman to love. For, by that strange law of reduplication which so often rules our life, the same circumstance was repeated with different actors; and

the proud, strong, handsome Anthony Harford
—this man of will, passion and adventure—
followed exactly the same line and trod in the
very footsteps of that ungainly Caleb Stagg, his
timid and discomfited predecessor. It remained
now to be seen whether the issue would be the
same or different.

'What can Harford be staying for at such a
place as Kingshouse?' said my lord when he
heard the news—like a man unable to see through
a millstone.

'For society. I daresay his own place is dull,'
said my lady—like a woman, having a reason
always ready.

'I should not think the "Kingshouse Arms" a
very lively look-out,' he returned.

'But he has us, and that compensates.'

'And he seems so much interested in astronomy,' said Lady Elizabeth with unconscious
diplomacy.

'So he does,' said her father; 'and now that
we have the frost again we will ask him to
dinner, and we can make a night of it up aloft.'

'You will freeze yourself to death some night

up aloft,' said the countess, just a point of querulousness—of quasi-grumbling—mingled with what else was care and consideration.

' Oh, we have wraps and mufflers, as you know,' was her husband's reply, not so grateful for the care as desirous to stave off the grumbling.

Both he and Lady Elizabeth were in riding costume. A ride with her father was one of her greatest pleasures, though her mother always expected to see her brought home on a shutter, living, as the poor lady did, in a chronic state of apprehension where she was afraid of everything.

' We will ride round by the town, and leave a message at the " Arms," ' continued the earl. ' I do not suppose he is engaged anywhere else.'

'I should think not,' said Lady Elizabeth, who was anxious he should be asked.

' Why, to whom should he be engaged ?' asked her mother in surprise. ' Society is not so numerous here as to ask him every day to dinner.'

' He might be to the Asplines,' said her daughter.

'Or the Clanricardes,' said the earl. 'He seemed monstrously taken with Mrs. Clanricarde the other night; and upon my soul she looked uncommonly handsome! I never saw her look better. She might have been one of her own ancestors at the Court of the Grand Monarque.'

'She is a very striking-looking woman certainly,' said Lady Kingshouse, who herself had her own 'cachet'—and knew that she had. 'But I don't think Mr. Harford so desperately "épris" as all that.'

She did not say what 'all that' meant, and no one asked.

'Ah, well, there's no saying! And there are the horses,' said Lord Kingshouse looking at the clock; 'just three minutes behind time. I shall speak to Master Figgins and ask what he means by it. He must not grow unpunctual, else he will have to find a new master. Come, Delight, let us be off.'

And with a nice little : 'Good-bye, old dear,' to his wife, the two left the room—and after a solemn : 'Behind time, Figgins,' to the coachman, were soon cantering briskly along the hard metallic road on their way to the town and the 'Kingshouse Arms.'

How beautiful the day was! Lady Elizabeth thought she had never seen such a perfect winter's day. The sky was as blue as the blue speedwells of spring, and the hoar-frost shone in the sun like so much pencilled fretwork wrought by the Sweet Spirit who gives the beetle its shining coat of green enamel and the butterfly its softer plumes. No moving life over the frozen fields or through the still air gave the sense of change. It was, so far, a dead world, crystallized into immortal loveliness—in a way unreal, and yet so beautiful—a world wherein the most fantastic images seemed natural and akin.

For the moment Lady Elizabeth forgot that other life in which she habitually dwelt—that life of suffering which she soothed, of sorrow which she shared. Breaking through that large envelope of sympathy by which her days were somewhat saddened, the high spirits natural to her age rippled up like an iridescent fountain; and she forgot that famine and misery and tears and wrong-doing stained the page of human history, and that the Messiahs must be crucified if they wish to redeem. Sweet she always was—thoughtful, unselfish, compassionate, sympathetic, but playful rarely—hilarious never. Now she laughed in that plenitude of girlish happiness which sees a cause for joy and a source of mirth in the most insignificant thing that passes. She talked and laughed, and was as radiant as those sun-lighted clouds which caught the gleam on their white fleeces, so that they dazzled the eyes which looked at them.

The earl scarcely knew his dear Delight in her new mood. It was as if the moon had suddenly blazed into the noonday sun—as if the dove had changed its tremulous call for the glad song of the lark—as if the waxen lily had blushed into the damask rose. It was all the brisk and frosty air, he thought, smiling with pleasure to see his darling so gay. There was nothing in the world so good for young people as plenty of open-air exercise—horse-exercise above all. He was so glad that he had assented to her proposal to ride together. He did not always assent when she asked. He would for the future, oftener.

Sitting square in her saddle, as if part and parcel of her horse—her cheeks flushed with the rapid ride and the frosty air—her eyes as bright as the sun, and as soft as they were bright—her air and manner full of the veritable splendour of youth, health, and good spirits—she rode through the little town whereof her father was the suzerain ; and everyone who saw her said: 'How fair Lady Elizabeth looks to-day!' Some added : 'My word! but she is a gay brave lass !' and some : 'Pity she doesn't get a husband while her beauty lasts !' But all agreed that, such as she was, she was as fine a young lady as ever stepped in shoe-leather, and he would have to go far who would better her.

They had time to take notes and make their boorish remarks, not boorishly intended, while she and her father stood at the door of the quaint old-fashioned little inn—that 'Rats' Castle,' as one irate visitor from London called it—and waited for Anthony's appearance. He was indoors, the servant said, but just going out. A horse was at the door. Sure enough, in a short time he came out, booted and spurred, ready for riding, and looking even handsomer than usual. There was a light in his face, a lustre in his deep-set searching eyes, a very dignity in his bearing beyond his ordinary self, though he had always those manly graces in abundance. He was what he himself would have said 'more alive' even than was his wont. And he was never only half vitalized, as so many are. What gave him this extra power—this additional vitality? Something spoke in his eyes when he looked at Lady Elizabeth. Was it something spoken to her personally? or was it that some thought animated him which went out to her as to all others? Was she the object or the subject? As happiness and youth and high spirits and some nameless chord of harmony laughed in every glance and sang in every word with her, so, with him, a man's secret passion and concentrated thought shone in his face and echoed in his voice. The two met on a different plane from the one whereon they had met before; and to her it seemed as if they stood nearer together. But to him they were immeasurably farther off. And yet he said to himself: ' I wish she was my sister.'

The three rode off together through the town, and the gossips perked up their heads and wagged them in sage deliberation. Perhaps the lady had not so far to go for her husband, after all; and they made a fine pair—that did they.

The ride was one of the most charming Lady Elizabeth had ever had. Really she had not given sufficient credit to the beauty of their country, beautiful as she had always thought it! To-day it was a kind of fairyland, and she half dreaded lest it should dissolve away like a vision wrought by a dream of the night. She seemed scarcely to know herself or the prosaic conditions of existence as they were. It was enchantment—all the enchantment of the frost and the fairies!

Then, all things ending in their turn, this delightful ride, too, came to an end. And there was no coda. Anthony was engaged to dinner both to-day and to-morrow and the next day, and the earl did not stretch out so far as the fourth. He did not say to whom, and naturally they did not ask. But when they parted at the fork—one road leading to the town and the other to the Dower House—the sun seemed to have suddenly set for Lady Elizabeth and the blue to have dropped out of the sky. The song of the lark in her heart was hushed; the rose had faded back into the moonlight colour of the lily; and the fantastic loveliness of the frosted tracery over the leaves and twigs and grass and hedges were as crystal tears, bringing to her mind the sorrows of the poor and what this hard weather meant for them. She became pale and silent, and the iridescent fountain sank once more beneath the surface of tender sadness through which it had broken.

'Why, Delight, you are quite pale and silent. Are you tired?' asked the earl, as he noticed the sudden drooping and the sudden pallor.

'I think I am a little, dear,' was her gentle reply.

'And yet we have not ridden so very far,' he said.

'No; but we have ridden fast,' she returned.

'And that comes to the same thing?'

'Yes,' she said, with more meaning than she knew.

To which he flung back a cheery kind of caress in his 'Poor poppet!'—half lost in his horse's ringing hoofs as they cantered on to the gates of home.

CHAPTER IX.

RECONNOITRING.

Mrs. Clanricarde was essentially clever. She understood differences and profited by mistakes. Her insight was as discriminating as her touch was delicate, and she neither confounded substances nor confused experiences. To Anthony Harford she adopted a new set of tactics altogether from those which she had used with Caleb Stagg. Kind, frank, hospitable, friendly, she was careful not to let the faintest shadow of a second intention appear. In her steady ignoring of her marriageable daughter, she ran just the semblance of a risk on her own account; and Anthony need not have been exceptionally vain to have believed that she was, as Lady

Kingshouse said, 'éprise' with him herself, so wholly did she absorb his conversation and, apparently, his attention. She sedulously kept Estelle in the background. She did not speak of her at all, and to her but rarely. She asked nothing of her that should show off her accomplishments; and it was Anthony himself who found out that she could sing sweetly and play divinely, and that her sketches were far beyond the amateur average.

Was this the woman who had, as Mrs. Aspline said, flung her daughter at the head of Tom, Dick and Harry?

Anthony's heart rose and sickened as he thought of this calumny, which he tried to banish from his mind and could not. He was too jealous by nature to bear patiently the thought that some one else had filled those sweet eyes with the longing tenderness of love—that any other man had coveted what he desired and meant to make his own—that this pearl of price, this precious treasure of delight, had been mutely offered to any man alive and had been rejected. No, he would not believe this. And all the more would he not, seeing how little the mother now put her forward; and yet he, Anthony Harford, was a better match in all ways, as a man and a fortune, than either a consumptive artist or an enriched miner!

Always apparently occupied with Mrs. Clanricarde, Anthony used to place himself where he could see Estelle—where he could watch her face, her hands, her hair, and how she moved, and see her as she was, perfectly natural and unembarrassed. Glad to be left alone, she did not see that she was being watched; and this new man—mother's latest craze and favourite —gave her no kind of distress. She played chess with her father, or watched him pondering over his elaborate 'patiences,' with the grace and ease of perfect tranquillity; and Mrs. Clanricarde, who saw the whole game far more clearly than that unlucky George of hers saw how to work his two packs into sequence, let things be as they were, and seemed as blind as she was clear-sighted.

Anthony, too, made no mistakes, and did not spoil his chances by precipitation. He showed none of that hunger for an answering love which repels far oftener than it incites. He damped down the fire that burnt in his veins, and did not let it show, even in his eyes. He watched Estelle, but not to her own consciousness; and what the mother saw she did not proclaim. Sometimes he brought her into the conversation by a sudden question, as he brought her father—and in exactly the same manner. Then, when she smiled as she looked up and answered him, she swept the very heart out of him, so that sometimes this strong man, who could face a grizzly in his lair and a dozen Indians on the war-path without turning a hair, quivered from head to foot, and was forced to keep silent for a moment lest his altered voice should betray him. He restrained himself, however, as with a hand of iron; and she, like some timid antelope coming down to the fountain to drink, came on and on to her doom, utterly unconscious of what was awaiting her at the end. To him this time of watching, of preparation, though painful in a way, had its luxury too. It was like planting a rare rose-tree with thoughtful care and deliberation. Not now, but soon, will it bear its allotted bloom. It is too early to expect it yet. All in its own time. And, meanwhile, the greater care bestowed now—the greater deliberation and forbearance—the more splendid the result and the grander the reward. Also, like all men sincerely in love, in spite of his masterful temperament and resolute will, Anthony was afraid. So long as he did not speak, and she had not answered, he was the potential master of his fate and the possessor of the prize. When once he had put the power out of his hands into hers—what would be the result? He would not think of failure; and yet the idea forced itself on his consciousness rather than on his clear thought. She might reject his love like a flower withered before it had been worn. And then what should he do? He could not compel what she did not grant; and the light of his life would be over. But he would not think of this. He was not accustomed to failure, and the resolute will which had carried him safely over many a bad pass in his life's way so far would stand him in stead now, in this—the most important and the least assured—the most disastrous if he failed, but the most glorious if he succeeded. As he would—as he knew that he would—the lover's craven terrors notwithstanding.

Speaking one evening of his relations with the Asplines, and how it was that he had come here on that business of the trusteeship, which he had taken over after his father's death—he chanced to mention Thorbergh as the name of the town, the district, where his place was—'Thrift, by Thorbergh,' as the postal direction ran.

Mrs. Clanricarde looked up at the name.

'Thorbergh, in Loamshire?' she asked with keen interest.

'Yes,' he answered. 'Do you know it?'

'George,' said Mrs. Clanricarde, forgetting to answer her guest; 'what do you think? Mr. Harford's place is near Thorbergh!'

'Never!' said George with his fatuous smile. 'What an extraordinary coincidence!'

'Where? In what?' asked Anthony, suddenly grave.

Like a flash there came into his face that watching, Red-Indian look of a man scenting danger—suspicious, wary, awake and on his guard. Nothing could have shown the inner nature of the man more openly than this look, merely because there was some connection between his present friends and his old home.

'Oh,' laughed Mrs. Clanricarde; 'there is no great mystery in it after all. Only at Thorbergh lives a certain Mrs. Latimer—the widow of a cousin of my husband's, on whose death we shall receive a small accession of income. That is all. She must be a very old woman by now—past eighty, George, is she not?—but she lives on as those annuitants always do; and I daresay she has a good ten years before her yet.'

She laughed again. She did her best to laugh easily and naturally, but the tone was sharp and the effort painful and apparent.

'Where does she live?' asked Anthony. 'Latimer—I seem to know that name.'

'At No. 3, Highstile Lane,' said George, with the patness of unpleasant perfectness.

'Oh, that's it!' returned Anthony. 'Highstile Lane belongs to me, and she is one of my tenants.'

'How very singular!' said Mrs. Clanricarde again; and this time her animation—her pleased air, was not forced. It was a link. And when one is in want of a chain, any link is better than none.

'I will go and look after her for you,' said Anthony, who also was glad of that link, slender as it was. 'Shall I call on her when I go back to Thrift and report on her condition?'

'Yes, do,' said Mrs. Clanricarde.

'It will be a satisfaction,' chimed in her husband.

'It certainly will,' said Anthony, looking at Estelle. 'It will keep me in your memory,' he added with the humility of love.

'We should scarcely need this to keep you there,' returned Mrs. Clanricarde kindly. 'We are not a very inconstant set here at Les Saules —not "volage" in any way. In fact, we are too humdrum altogether for the present day. But I so much dislike the modern fast fashion! I prefer to be humdrum rather than of the period.'

'You could not be better than you are,' said Anthony, still looking at Estelle. 'I reckon those are nighest being right who are likest you; and the farther they are off your pattern the less they are to be admired.'

'Do they teach flattery in America?' asked Estelle's mother smiling.

'No, but they teach a man to speak as he thinks,' said Estelle's admirer, also smiling. 'Say, Miss Clanricarde, is that the right thing to do?'

'What?' asked Estelle, waking from a kind of dream.

She was watching her father's game, on the ordering and success of which she had secretly staked some portion of her hope. The king of hearts stood with her for Charlie, while she was the queen of spades; and how the two suits came, and by what difficulties and conditions these two special cards were surrounded, was an earnest of the future, as it had been countless times before. For is there any inanity, any folly devisable by man to which lovers will not give themselves, and in which they will not place serious faith when fate looks sour and happiness is so far off as to be invisible, perhaps for ever unattainable? Just then the fortunes of the game and the fate of these two painted symbols interested Estelle far more than her mother's new friend, who indeed did not interest her at all.

'Is it right to speak as we think?' Anthony asked again.

'Surely!' said Estelle. Then, with a rapid glance at her mother, she qualified her bolder assertion with a more cautious: 'At least I suppose so—sometimes.'

Like all timid people, she was afraid of a sudden question. She did not know what snares might not be woven out of the most innocent-looking material. She had been so often entrapped in this manner by her mother that she was perhaps justified now in her fear, and her hatred of the 'Socratic method' was not unnatural.

'I wonder if we do—any of us?' said Mrs. Clanricarde, with her philosophizing air, very charming and very false.

'As much as we can, I reckon,' said Anthony; but his philosophy smacked of the backwoods, not the drawing-room. 'It would be rather hot if we said all we thought at all times. We'd raise Cain, and that's a fact!'

'Discretion is sometimes the better part of valour,' said that foolish George, a little wide of the immediate point, as he always was.

'And we have good-breeding to consider,' put in Mrs. Clanricarde, still mildly philosophical.

'And the policy of waiting,' said Anthony with a sudden gleam in his eyes that made the watching mother's heart leap for joy at the meaning of its light.

'Yes, waiting,' she said quietly. '"All comes to him who knows how to wait." That is a French proverb, and a true one.'

'All?' asked Anthony with emphasis.

'All,' she repeated, also with emphasis.

Estelle looked at her mother. Her look was as swift and its meaning was as subtle as on the day when she and that mother went together to the wood and she had glanced to see if the road was clear. And Anthony caught that swift flash to-night as her mother had caught it then. It stirred him with again a sudden movement of jealousy and suspicion. There was more in it than he understood, and it implied a something shared between mother and daughter which filled him with angry apprehension.

'Then you think, too, that all comes to him who knows how to wait?' he asked, speaking to Estelle with a strange little touch of sternness in his voice.

'I do not know. It is to be hoped it does,' she replied, not raising her eyes. 'Now, dear,' she added suddenly to her father; 'you have spoiled the game. You cannot do it if you put the king of clubs there over the queen of spades.'

'I will try. I think I can work it,' said that foolish George, who at 'patience,' as with his investments, could never see an inch before him, and who always thought that he could work the most impossible combinations.

'The game is lost!' said Estelle with a sigh.

The king of hearts was hemmed in so as to be useless, and the queen of spades could not be moved because of the king of clubs, which blocked her in. And that fierce, square-shouldered Bluebeard of the pack suddenly looked to Estelle like Anthony Harford.

'Shall I try to straighten it out?' asked Anthony, coming to the table.

'You cannot,' said Estelle, rising and leaving it.

'Do you play this game?' asked Mr. Clanricarde, still fingering the cards and trying to remove the irremovable block.

'Oh, I play pretty nigh every game in the pack,' said Anthony; 'but these one-handed concerns are beyond me. And I do not think I should care for them.'

'They are very interesting when you know them,' said Mr. Clanricarde.

'I prefer an antagonist,' said Anthony.

'You have an antagonist,' returned the other. 'Fortune and your own want of skill and foresight.'

Anthony laughed.

'My own want of skill and foresight!' he said. 'I don't own up to that! I'll play with my skill and foresight against fortune or any other odds you like. But, want of skill! I reckon that's not in the schedule!'

'Take care, pride goes before a fall,' said that foolish George, in exactly the same words as Mrs. Aspline had used.

Anthony tossed up his head like a horse unduly checked.

'I'll follow my pride and risk the fall,' he said, with a certain outburst of temper that made Mrs. Clanricarde say to herself: 'That man wants careful handling. He will stand no nonsense;' and Estelle to think suddenly, not of dear, sweet, darling Charlie, strange to say, but of that patient, good, unselfish, and ungainly omadhaun who held her as a queen.

Soon after this Anthony took his leave and went back to the 'Kingshouse Arms' as if possessed by seven devils—he did not clearly know why.

CHAPTER X.

'I AM GLAD.'

LET those who can explain this seeming contradiction. The longer Anthony Harford remained at Kingshouse, and the stronger grew his
passion for Estelle, the farther off he seemed
from its expression. She had the strangest
power of chilling him, so that he could not
speak to her tenderly, nor even look at her with
that unmistakable meaning which love flings
like so much golden light into a man's eyes.
An invisible but insurmountable barrier seemed
to rise up between them when they were together, but he could not say where it began nor
what was its name. Something mysterious,
impenetrable—an atmosphere like that of a

spell—surrounded her and froze him into silence. Then he would rage at himself and her,
when he had left her—swear that to-morrow
this cursed game should end, when he would
make her see his mind, and in seeing his would
bend her own—that he would offer his love and
compel her to accept it and give him hers in
return. And when to-morrow came the whole
thing was renewed. The spell was cast over
him as before, and he burnt with that internal
fever which expresses itself in the glacial and
shivering outside. For another day he was
silently repelled and sensibly controlled; and
for yet another day Estelle was free.

This fierce turmoil in Anthony's heart began
to show itself in his looks. The bronzed face,
so dark and clear-skinned, was becoming fur-
rowed and livid; the steadfast eyes were now
more fierce than steadfast, and their quiet
watching had passed into acute suspicion; the
strength, which had once been the main expression of the face, was translating itself into a
kind of tormented and suppressed ferocity; and
he looked like a man overwrought and for the

moment overbalanced. He looked indeed as he felt, possessed by demons; and he was as he looked. He would have given worlds for one hour of the rude, rough life of the far west, when he could have made a quarrel which would have ended in bowie-knives and revolvers. He longed to horsewhip Mr. Medlicott for that little offence which still rankled; and each man felt that the new-comer was decidedly dangerous and to be gently entreated if a row was to be avoided. It was a new reading of his character—a new side turned to the world of Kingshouse; and all saw the change, though none understood the cause.

The only house to which Anthony often went —always excepting Les Saules—was the Dower House. He divided his time pretty equally between these two places, gathering poison at the one and its antidote at the other. The only real comfort he knew was when he was with Lady Elizabeth and her people. The Asplines exasperated him past bearing, and the rest of the world half maddened him. They were all as unreal as so many gibbering ghosts, and

he could not endure their inanities in the terrible
contest going on within him. But Lady Elizabeth was the David to his Saul; and she, who
knew nothing—though she sometimes half dis-
cerned, as in a dream, and then sank deeper
into sleep and knew no more—she was glad to
see the evident tranquillity that came over him
after he had been with her for a short time. He
came to the Dower House, haggard and moody
and burning with that internal fever—that suppressed ferocity—which made him verily like a
soul in pain. And after he had sat with her
for half-an-hour, talking of things which perhaps touched him more nearly than she knew,
and which, because they touched him, stirred
her also more deeply than he knew—he grew
quiet and calm, and was evidently mentally
soothed and spiritually restored. She could
not refuse to see that his regained tranquillity
was due to her own moral influence, which
flowed over him like so much balm over a
wound, and exorcised the demons within as by
the blessed sprinkling of holy water. She had
never taken such joy in that gift of spiritual

healing which she knew she possessed as she did now, when Anthony Harford came to her in bitter pain and left her in contented calm.

'If I could love her!' he often thought. 'She would have been the fit wife for me, if that other had not bewitched me. If I could love her! But it is too late now. The die is cast. I will hold Estelle in my arms as my wife, or I will kill her first and then myself!'

Meanwhile Estelle held fast by her faith in Charlie; and, without one overt look or word that her mother could take hold of, spread that spell over Anthony which froze him into silence and reduced him to that state which was like to a geyser under a glacier. She knew that if things should come to an open declaration they could not be so easily managed as with poor Caleb. She had different material to work with here, and material that was stronger than herself. She scarcely knew what she proposed to herself. She only felt that each day passed without that dreaded summons to surrender, was a gain, and that hope of some indeterminate and unnamed kind always coloured the dawning of to-morrow. She did not know that she should escape. She hoped so, and she meant to try her best; but she did not know.

Just at this juncture Charlie Osborne suddenly ceased to write to her. She heard nothing of him and knew nothing. His last letter had been from Yokohama, when he said to her that he had looked up at the stars and thought of her—more beautiful than any in the sky. After this came down that dull blank curtain of silence which in itself is a kind of death.

At first Estelle suspected her mother of the time-honoured trick of intercepting her letters. But though Mrs. Clanricarde was quite capable of this or any other ruse which diplomacy consecrates to the use of wire-pullers, in this special instance she was guiltless. So Estelle found; for she herself met the postman and opened the bag before she brought it into the room; and not a letter from Charlie, and not a line of news brought her either comfort or despair. Soon the mystery was solved. A letter come from Lawrence Smythe Smith which told the whole sad story. Charlie Osborne was sick unto death at

Yokohama, and the yacht had to come home and leave him there in hospital. But the letter added he was in good hands, and would be well looked after; and his friends at Kingshouse were not to feel alarmed. He himself had desired this letter to be written to Mrs. Clanricarde, who was adjured to break the news gently to Estelle, and to be good to his darling—always his one adored and faithfully beloved!

Here, then, was a loophole, for which Mrs. Clanricarde was sorrowfully grateful. Of course she was sorry. You cannot hear of the dangerous illness of a handsome young creature you have known all his life, and not be moved in that part of your nature which goes by the name of bowels of compassion. But also she was grateful for the possible, and it would seem more than probable chance, that the great obstacle to Estelle's success in life would soon be removed —when her future would be clear and her heart once more a 'tabula rasa,' save for an insignificant little scar of no account. She would be very good to her, very tender, very sympathetic. And so she was. She told her the sad news with really admirable softness of manner and undeclared, but implied, sympathy. And she did not fall foul of the headache which kept the poor girl invisible in the afternoon when Anthony Harford called, and sent her to bed before her usual time to make that headache decidedly worse by weeping. So much consideration did this careful mother give to natural feeling, and so warily was she walking—warned by her former mistake.

Unable to see Estelle, Anthony rode off to the Dower House for Lady Elizabeth, and was comforted to find that she was at home. In his irritated and secretly furibond state, he half suspected the headache to mean disinclination to see him; and for the first time seemed to hear a false ring in Mrs. Clanricarde's shrill French voice. But suspicion does no good when proofs are wanting, and Anthony had to be satisfied with what was given him and to ride away as if content. Then he came to the Dower House to lay himself, as it were, in the hands and on the knees of this sweetest daughter of the gods, this modern maiden representative of Hestia, the All

Mother. How deeply he revered her—how tenderly he admired her!

'You are scarce like a woman to me,' he said to her to-day. 'You are more like one of those beautiful pagan goddesses run into the mould of an English young lady!'

She laughed a little shyly and coloured with embarrassment and pleasure combined.

'The old goddesses were rather vague and vapoury creatures,' she said, speaking in the air as people do who have to say something when their breast is throbbing, and their brain confused in consequence.

'I know some like to them,' said Anthony, thinking of Estelle; 'as vague, as vapoury, as unattainable.'

'Short of crying for the moon what is un-attainable?' she asked, thinking neither of Estelle nor of herself. The one was out of the field altogether. The other—she had not put the question to herself, but deep down in the hidden wells of her inner consciousness, she knew that this other was not unattainable. She answered him with a question then, that had no direct personal reference; yet it brought the colour still more to her face, and when she had said it she wished she had not spoken.

'Should be to a man—nothing,' said Anthony. 'In active life there would be nothing, if he were strong and knew his alphabet. But when you come to woman—and how she is to be approached and how she is to be won—the scene changes; and what he has learned in the camp doesn't quite serve him in the drawing-room.'

'It depends on the woman,' said Lady Elizabeth.

'Do you believe in magic?' he asked abruptly.

'No,' she answered. 'Surely not! Do you?'

'I don't quite know,' he answered. 'A month or so ago I would have shouted 'No' with the loudest; but now—I scarce know what to think.'

There was a pause. Then Lady Elizabeth said in rather a low voice:

''I don't quite know to what you are alluding—so I cannot really answer you. I cannot touch your point.'

'Oh, it's of no consequence,' he answered with a strange commingling of carelessness and desperation. 'But I feel as if a spell had been cast over me somehow. To try and not succeed—to be dumb when you wish to speak—to be unable to show even what is in your heart and mind—to feel baffled and prevented and off the trail altogether—what is that, Lady Elizabeth? Seems to me like magic, somehow, to a man like myself, who never shirked a danger and never funked it when it came.'

' But are you in that state ?' she asked, raising her eyes in wonder.

Conscious of the broad sympathies between them she could not take this to herself. It was a state touching some one else—something that she did not know.

' Yes,' he said a little sullenly.

Again there was silence, so dead that it seemed as if the very air was frozen and could not be moved.

'I should not think you could be baffled in anything, if you once fully determined to succeed,' she then said, speaking with the effort of one lifting a heavy weight—breaking through a strong enclosure.

His face brightened.

'You think not,' he said.

'No,' she answered.

'And you advise me to persevere—to over-come the spell—to be master of myself and of fate?'

She turned as pale as the linen strip about her throat. She was conscious that she was looking into unknown depths and standing on the brink of an unfathomed pool.

'Yes,' she said. 'Persevere.'

He got up and took her hands in both of his.

'I will remember your advice,' he said, press-ing them hard, while his eyes looked down into her face with unutterable tenderness—unspeak-able gladness. 'If I come to my happiness it will be through you and by you.'

How he loved and reverenced this fair and saintly counsellor at this moment! How deeply he loved her! She felt his tenderness, his love, as it might have been the sudden effulgence of the sun, and all her heart went out to him, as a flower that opened to the light.

'Now you know my secret,' he said; 'and now you can judge what 1 feel—and feel for me. And you will know what I owe to you when the time comes.'

He drew her hands up to his breast and kissed them with the most loving, the most reverent tenderness. But for her habit of self-coutrol she would have flung herself into his arms to have offered him of her own free will more than he had claimed. But she remembered in good time that he had not said the one decisive, irrevocable word, and she refrained.

' If I win her,' he said again, ' it will be thanks to you who have heartened me. Estelle's almost sister now, you will be my true sister then, and our happiness will be yours. God bless you, best and dearest of friends. You do not know what you have done for me !'

For a moment the earth reeled under Lady Elizabeth's feet, and she knew nothing of time or space, or life itself, save the one sharp consciousness of pain. Then, with a supreme effort

—the effort of a martyr at the stake who prays and does not cry—she said, in a strange and level voice:

'I am glad.'

And Anthony believed her.

CHAPTER XI.

MR. LATIMER'S WIDOW.

ONE of Mrs. Clanricarde's many troubles, poor uneasy soul! was the obstinate existence of that Mrs. Latimer, now domiciled at Thorbergh in one of Anthony Harford's houses, spoken of in a former chapter. She was an old woman who had what Caroline Fox called the 'ugly trick of living.' She had already outlived the allotted span by full ten years, and by all accounts she was good for double that extra allowance. She neither tumbled downstairs nor set fire to her cap; neither fell into the grate nor got bronchitis unawares—according to the general rule with old people, whom death desires to take and life does not care to keep; and the clergyman, who vouched for her being still in the body when quarter-day came round and her income was due, made no marginal remarks comforting to those hungry watchers who were waiting for her well-worn shoes. For the death of this persistent old lady would enrich the much-tried household of Les Saules by just eight hundred a-year. And really, when one is in such direful straits as were the Clanricardes at this moment, eight hundred a-year, less income-tax, is equal to a thousand to those round whose door no black-muzzled wolf is prowling, and within whose golden reservoir no drought makes itself felt. And the money would be safe when it should come; for which wise provision on the part of Andrew Latimer Mrs. Clanricarde was well inclined to forgive him all the rest. It was strictly tied up against the possibility of any disastrous handling by that unlucky George, who else would be sure to let it all slip through his fingers as if each five-pound note were a live eel from the brook. Had he the power of handling it he would as surely make ducks-and-drakes of it as he had already made those fearful wild fowl of his own, under the idea that he was multiplying it by just so many ricochets as he got out of each sovereign. When it should come, therefore, it would be sure. But the question was: When would it come?

Mrs. Latimer was the widow of a cousin of Mr. Clanricarde's who had died about ten years ago; leaving only his relict to enjoy for her lifetime, but no children to divide his modest fortune after her death. George Clanricarde had always been a favourite of his, since the days when the one had been a man grown, and the other was only a neat, affectionate, cocky little lad at school. And the friendship had continued after the neat little boy had become the dapper young man, as weak as water and as obstinate as weak people generally are, but always affectionate and well-meaning—ruining himself and all he loved with the best and kindest intentions in the world. When, however, Cousin Latimer, then quite an elderly man, chose to marry a certain Miss Stone, of whom no one had ever heard—of whose birth, parentage, education, and antecedents nothing whatever was known—then, mainly owing to the intervention of Mrs. Clarincarde, who resented this introduction of a stranger with possible infants to follow, as a wrong done to poor George's expectations, there had been but little intercourse between the former friends and chums. The Latimers had lived in London, the Clanricardes at Kingshouse; and the interests of peace were best preserved by keeping personally apart, and satisfying the diminished sentiment by letters. And not even when it was known that Mrs. Latimer was even older than her husband—a quinquagenarian when he married, and a septuagenarian when he died—and that George had been left chief inheritor after her death, not even then was Mrs. Clanricarde appeased to the point of reconciliation with 'that woman.' Hence, neither she nor her husband had ever seen her, nor knew of what manner of person she was.

There was one slight link between the houses, but it was a very slight one. It was simply this. A Kingshouse woman, one Mary Crosby, who had been Charlie Osborne's nurse and who had lived with the vicar's family till Mr. Osborne died, was now Mrs. Latimer's servant. She had first nursed Mr. Latimer on his death-bed, and had then continued in her place as his widow's attendant. After the old gentleman's death, her own mother, also a widow, had removed to London from Kingshouse to be near her daughter. And with this ended the Crosby relations with their old home. No one ever heard of them again, save that Mrs. Crosby was dead, and that Mary still went on taking care of the old lady. And she took care of her so faithfully that Mrs. Latimer lived in perfect health and well-being, and showed no sign as yet of an accommodating departure. So that Mrs. Clanricarde was well-nigh a-weary with her continual query, to which came never a response : 'When will that dreadful old woman die ?' Mrs. Crosby, a hale, hearty woman, fifteen years her junior, had slipped quietly off to the shades below; but this terrible impediment—this apparently immortal annuitant—still clung to her chair at life's crowded table, and ate the bread which by now should have satisfied, not to say disagreed with her—and which should have been handed on to the inheritors standing so close to her coveted seat.

There was no help for it. Whenever George wrote to the trustees he received for answer a copy of the certificate sent by the clergyman, who vouched for having seen and talked to Mrs. Mary Latimer on such and such a date, when he had found her in apparent good health and perfect sanity of mind. Unless, then, Mrs. Clanricarde was prepared to go and strangle the old obstructive with her own hands, she had to put up with the 'ugly trick,' and to wait with such patience as she could command until the slow pace of time should bring to her that inheritance so greatly coveted.

Meanwhile, about ten or eleven years ago—just after Mrs. Crosby died—the old lady left London and took a house on the outskirts of the village of Thorbergh—that village where Thrift was one of the gentleman's houses which enabled the scanty trade to live. One of Anthony Harford's tenants, she was also one of his most satisfactory—paying her rent with praiseworthy punctuality—never asking for a set-off on account of repairs—never asking for something to be done to the drains, for a new kitchen range, nor for another kind of cistern—seeming to desire nothing so much as peace and the absence of all causes for contention.

She was a very quiet old lady, and she lived the life of a recluse.   She never went out, and by reason of her infirmities she could not manage to go to church.   But the clergyman went to see her, in his ministerial capacity, regularly once a month ; when she and her servant listened to his prayers with great devoutness, and were evidently all the better spiritually for his ministrations.   Save this clergyman of the parish, this Mr. Trotter who vouched for her continued existence, Mrs. Latimer saw no one —living mostly in the back parlour which gave on to the little garden, and denied to the neighbours when they called.   She was faithfully and assiduously served by a tall, well-dressed, well-looking, but very resolute woman of about forty or thereabouts ; who evidently had her interests at heart as much as if they had been her own. She did all the marketing; paid the bills; spoke to few, made friends with none; and was as stiff and stand-off as a grenadier. When she was out it was in vain to rap or ring at No. 3, Highstile Lane. The old lady was surely as deaf as a post or as lame as a log, for she neither answered through the keyhole nor opened on the chain, and the place was like a tomb till the servant came back. About twice a year the two concocted a letter to Charles Osborne, Esq., which seemed to give them great satisfaction to write. It gave Master Charlie just as great to receive. It was always an un-signed letter, and it always contained bank notes. It was the anonymous contribution to his meagre income alluded to before; and it was sent by Mary Crosby, his former nurse, and now the devoted attendant of Mrs. Latimer, George Clanricarde's cousin by marriage.

The old lady lived very simply. For a lady, as she was, or ought to be, she lived meagrely and dressed poorly, though she was always noticeably clean and tidy. Of that eight hundred a-year she certainly did not spend over two, all told. But she made no response to the clergyman's leading questions as to her mode of life, and why she had arranged her expenditure on such a much lower scale than might have been expected, and expressed herself thoroughly satisfied with all its conditions.

She kept only this one servant, Mary, and she wanted none other, she said. She could not be better done by if she had a dozen; and she did not care to keep a pack of idle hussies eating their heads off and doing nought but gad after the lads. She was best with just their two selves, now that her master—that is, her husband —had died. Men were fashious, and had to be provided for, but she had always liked a quiet life. At her age, indeed, she was only fit to bide by the chimney corner thinking of her latter end and praising God for all His mercies. Though she enjoyed good health, the Lord be praised, she was not a young woman now— eighty-one last birthday. And, however hale and stout she might be for her years, eighty- one is eighty-one, when all's said and done, and one cannot make it a day less by wishing.

And when she said this she invariably coughed, that old woman's decided 'hoast,' that 'church-yard cough,' which seemed to come up from her list slippers, and which would have reassured Mrs. Clanricarde had she heard it through the partition—as Mary did.

She spoke with a strong provincial accent—stronger than might have been expected in a gentleman's widow. But that was not so extra-ordinary after all. The marriage had been a mésalliance—as Mr. Trotter had heard from the Clanricardes; and the aged so often revert to the first conditions of their life, and double back on the long-left ground of childhood, forgetting the lessons learned in the middle distance. So that perhaps there was nothing very remark-able in this clean and tidy old lady's broad Northern accent, for all that she was the widow of a gentleman and in receipt of a pleasant little income of eight hundred a year. What was more remarkable was her wonderful fresh-ness and vitality. At eighty-one years of age, she did not look over sixty-five at the outside, and hale at that. To be sure her hair was of that strangely snowy white which one sees so often in American women of about forty, or even younger—hair as absolutely free from colour of any kind as those white lilacs which are grown in the dark, of which the petals are like so much snow. Her hands, however, were plump, and with none of the starting veins nor cord-like sinews of old age; and her arms and shoulders were still firm of flesh and strong in the muscles. Her black, sharp, twinkling eyes betrayed a vitality simply marvellous at her age. They were undimmed by any of those white spots or by that fatal 'arcus senilis' inherent to old age. They were eyes which could take in a joke and laugh back a jesting reply—eyes to which even a likely lad might find something to say, and not throw away his time—they were eyes which, coupled with the firm and solid flesh, were really remarkable in so old a lady; and Ninon de l'Enclos herself could not have had brighter. On the whole, she was a wonderful specimen of her sex, and to all appearance there was no reason why she should

not live to the magic age of a hundred, or
even beyond, and see the hungry watchers
'happed up' in the churchyard before her. As
it was, she made them suffer the pains of Tanta-
lus in Hades. Nor was she herself quite free
from apprehension. There was something that
did not quite suit her in her life, as she had it;
and yet—what could it be?

'I'm always glad, Mary, when quarter-day
has come and gone,' said the old lady one day
to her servant, after the usual formalities had
been gone through—when Mr. Trotter had come
to duly examine and report on the continued
existence of Mrs. Mary Latimer, relict of Andrew Latimer, gentleman, late of Harley Street,
London, and now of No. 3, Highstile Lane,
Thorbergh, and had found her of sound mind
and body, and the fit and proper recipient of
that trimestral two hundred pounds.

'Hoot!' said Mary. 'There's no occasion.
Everything is just as it should be, and nobody's
a penny the wiser.'

'It's a queer feeling,' said Mrs. Latimer. 'I
sometimes misdoubt myself.'

'Misdoubt yourself of what?' queried Mary sharply. 'That you *are* Mrs. Latimer?'

'My word, lass, but you are a staunch 'un!' said the old lady with a little laugh.

'There's not much good in being slack,' returned the younger woman. 'What we've undertaken to do that we have to stick to, and we have Scripture warrant for not looking back when we've put our hand to the plough.'

'Yes,' said Mrs. Latimer a little drily. 'But maybe our plough is one the Scriptures wouldn't much hold with.'

'And why not?' asked Mary. 'Not to do the good you do? What would become of that blessed Master Charlie but from the help he gets from his friend unbeknown—Mrs. Latimer, of Thorbergh? And, I ask, why shouldn't we, as had to bear the heat and burden of the day, have our reward when we have worked so hard for it?'

'Ay, we have worked hard,' said Mrs. Latimer. 'And it was a shame that the master never so much as left a five-pound note after you had done all that you did do for him.'

'I have taken my change out of him for it,' said Mary with quiet grimness. 'Folk should think twice before they do unjustly and made enemies in this world. One never knows when one's sin may not find one out and the one as we've trampled on rise up in judgment against us.'

'No,' said Mrs. Latimer; but she spoke with a cough and a little uneasily; and Mary, saying: 'You'll be wanting your tea, Mrs. Latimer,' bustled out of the room, bringing the conversation to a close.

'It'll all come to light some day,' said the old lady, resuming her eternal knitting. 'It was a rash thing to do; but the temptation was great, and Mary, she's that strong-headed there's no going counter to her. But she's over bold and confident, is Mary, and doesn't seem to think or fear. I'd like to know the end of it for my part, and what the sentence would be. I fancy it would be pretty heavy. But Mary says there's no chance, and I don't see any great fear myself. Still, it's sure to come out, if not one day then another, and I'd get out of it afore if I had the chance. But I don't very well see how that can be. I'm glad we have that tidy lot saved and put away there in the bed-tick. No banks for me, not if I know it, with their managers and directors and trash, who go off with the brass and leave the dupes to starve. A good bit of stout cloth, well sewed with waxed thread and hid among the feathers—that's my style; and it's the best, I reckon, out of the lot! And while it's there we can just make ourselves scarce if things look like Queer-street, and our room would be better than our company. But it's a venture-some thing to do, and I oft wonder at myself. And really, if it were not for Master Charles, I think I'd be fit to give up any day of the year. But that bonny bairn holds me to it, little as he knows what's being done for him or who's a-doing it. Lord love him! The last time I saw him and he gave me that kiss, he took the heart out of me; and I said to myself then: " Ye bonny little lad, if ever I can do you a good turn I will," and I've stuck to my word even on to this, and will to the end, that will I!'

Here Mary brought in the tea, and Mrs. Latimer's musings came to an end.

This, then, was the annuitant whom Anthony Harford had promised Mrs. Clanricarde he would see to report on her condition, which the impecunious wife of that unlucky George—the ill-starred mother of that perverse Estelle—hoped would be as full of evil circumstances as were compatible with life and prophetic of speedy death. But he would not go to see her yet, being still under the spell at Kingshouse—waiting to see how things would turn—whether he should have to live down that fever or finally be enabled to slake it at the sometimes too satisfying, too refrigerating fount of matrimony —that sometimes grave of love, into which, however, love must needs descend. If Mrs. Latimer and Mary had known that at this present moment their landlord was at Kingshouse, dining with the residuary legatee, George Clanricarde—watching, studying Estelle, whom Charlie Osborne loved and who loved Charlie— while giving his soul as a habitation for seven devils to possess because he saw just the nameless and formless shadow of that love cast athwart his own path—if they had known of all those links now being forged between them and their past—them and their future—even stout-hearted Mary would have quailed, and the vivacious black eyes of the old lady would have become dim with fear. But nothing being known, nothing was foreseen. Anthony remained at Kingshouse; Mrs. Latimer drew her quarterly allowance; Charlie Osborne, who had studied the stars from the streets of Yokohama, now tossed in fever in the hospital; Estelle wrote to him long letters of constant love and gentle trust; and Mrs. Clanricarde, taught by experience, walked warily and made no mistake.

CHAPTER XII.

THE GRAND COUP.

'AT Yokohama, of fever, Charles, the only son of the Rev. James Osborne, late vicar of Kingshouse.' This was the announcement in the *Times* which Mrs. Clanricarde read first—Mr. Clanricarde having taken the whole inside, telegrams, leading articles and the money market, leaving to his wife the advertisements and the 'dead and alive.' This was almost the only privilege of his sex which that unlucky George dared to claim. For all the rest his wife came first, and her will ruled where his yielded.

Mrs. Clanricarde read the announcement without the quivering of a muscle or the turning of a hair. She read it, indeed, as if she had expected it, and looked over the top of the page at her daughter, speculating on her reception of the thunder-bolt which neither surprised nor shocked herself. Estelle was eating her luncheon, ignorant of and not foreseeing the blow that was about to fall. No presentiment warned her now, nor had any foreshadowed her coming sorrow. The Psychical Society could have made nothing of her. She had had no dream of Charlie—pale, tearful, looking at her with eyes full of a mournful farewell. No vision had passed before her, halting for a moment to fill her heart with the pain and terror of love. No voice calling her name in the dear accents so well known had sounded in her ear. No dog had howled in warning. No owl had hooted ghastly presage. Full of sorrow and pity for this illness which had struck down her beloved, she had also the buoyant belief of youth, and felt sure that he would recover. For to love, life is immortality, and the beloved cannot die.

At this moment she was not thinking of anything very definitely. She was only dumbly conscious, as always now, of Anthony Harford and her ever-increasing difficulties himward. She knew that the net was drawing daily tighter and closer around her; and that the repelling, almost mesmeric power, she had over him would one day be broken through to her dread and danger. She was conscious that she would have at last to hear what she had so long restrained. Yet she meant to make a good fight of it, and to appeal to his generosity as she had already appealed to Caleb Stagg's. But she was more than doubtful of the result. The masterful will and hard-mouthed resoluteness of Anthony made a man of a very different mould from Caleb Stagg in his lowly humility and tender self-abnegation. Anthony would marry the woman he fancied, however reluctant she might be; supremely confident that he could distance every other rival, and wipe out every other thought or affection, when once he had her as his own and could woo her as he would. He was a man who owned no superior, and whose master had yet to be born. What he set his hand to do, that would he eventually accomplish—the most formidable obstacles counting no more than so many straws in his way. And a woman's love ranked with the rest. Whatever moments of depression and doubt he might have, the central thread remained unbroken—the woman he loved he would have, and the woman he had should love him.

All this Estelle felt rather than formularized. Still, she meant to make a good fight of it. And perhaps she would, after all, succeed. How could a man marry a girl whose love was another's, and who said frankly she could never love him and would always hate him, if even he took her by force? He could not! To Estelle the very idea was sacrilege; and Anthony Harford, though self-willed, was not sacrilegious. Yet even if he were, and even if he should insist on this crime, there was always one door left open—she could run away. She had money, got in a mysterious manner, and really Charlie's, not hers. That did not much matter. The tie between them was so intimate—their lives were so thoroughly fused together—that no shame attached to her using his money for her own preservation from an unholy marriage. Bank-notes, crisp and clean, sent, he never knew nor could discover by whom, came two or three times a year to him. They were addressed to the Post Office, Kingshouse, and their receipt was given in the *Times* under the initials 'C. O.' When Charlie went to London the letters were forwarded to him in due course from the office. When he went abroad, he empowered Estelle to receive them and to keep the money as a future provision for themselves. She had done so; and she had sent the acknowledgments to the paper as she had been instructed. And now she had close on two hundred pounds, which would help her to the maintenance of her integrity if pushed to the last resource. It would be a desperate step to take; and she trembled when she thought of it, as she often did, realizing the shame and scandal and disgrace of her flight, and the blow it would be to her mother. But if needs must she would. She would do anything rather than marry Anthony Harford—with Charlie at Yokohama, looking across the seas, trusting in her constancy, and waiting for renewed health to embark and claim her. She would feel herself guilty of a shameful crime were she to marry another while her own true love and promised husband lived. Not all the vows said before the altar—not all the blessings pronounced by the priest—nor the iron links forged by the law and demanded by society, could make her feel other than an adulteress were she to yield herself to insistance—whether her mother's or Anthony Harford's. She was Charlie's and none other's; and during his life no other man should own her.

If she was thinking at all, she was thinking all this, but she was feeling rather than thinking, and quietly eating her somewhat slender luncheon :—as we all must eat, poor slaves of matter as we are, let what will betide!

Still holding the paper in her hand, Mrs. Clanricarde called Estelle to come with her into the drawing-room. She had put on a mask of sorrow, and the girl saw that something was amiss. Her mind swept rapidly round the narrow circle of distant friends, but the very immensity of her fear excluded the worst for

Charlie. Love deals so gently with suspicion in all its forms! When a friend hints at a fault, you do not suppose a crime; when a child falls ill, the mother does not foresee death. Were it otherwise, love would be a burden too great to be borne, and the heart would be crushed like Tarpeia beneath its golden weight.

'My dear, I have bad news for you,' began Mrs. Clanricarde, with great tenderness and sympathy of voice and manner.

'What is it, mother?' asked Estelle, her soft eyes opened wide and dark as the sunless night.

'You must be brave, my dear,' she returned. 'It will be a heavy blow to you. Poor Charlie!

'What is it, mother?' asked Estelle again, with preternatural calmness. She seemed as if struck to stone, pale and rigid as a statue.

'Ah, poor boy! I am so grieved for him and for you, my dear,' said Mrs. Clanricarde, softly.

She pressed her handkerchief to her eyes.

'Mother, what is it?' repeated Estelle with the strange sternness of great and sudden fear.

She laid her hand on her mother's arm and

unconsciously gripped it till she nearly caused her to shriek for pain.

'He is gone, dear!' said Mrs. Clanricarde; 'gone home to heaven, where he will never suffer more!'

'It is not true,' said Estelle. 'He could not have died without coming to tell us. He could not!'

Her mother gave her the paper.

'Here is the announcement,' she said. 'I know no more than you.'

Estelle looked at it. Her large eyes were opened wide, her lips were parched, her brain was all confused and as if on fire. The letters seemed to form themselves into individual and living creatures, which had each its own physiognomy; and then they were like the clanging of bells sounding in her ears:—'At Yokohama, of fever, Charles, the only son of the Rev. James Osborne, late vicar of Kingshouse.' It was a kind of dirge or chant which seemed to fill all space with sound, flowing out from that point where the letters turned to living creatures on the paper—showing to her eyes what the bells sounded to her ears. There was not a tear, not a sob, not a sigh—only this dry, wide-eyed statuesque horror of attention, like one looking into the grave of the beloved.

Her mother spoke to her; she did not hear. She put her arm round the stiffened shoulders; she did not feel.

'Estelle! Estelle!' she said; 'speak to me, dear. Estelle, ma chérie, speak!'

The girl looked at her mother at first as if she did not know her; then she shuddered and pushed that mother from her with a movement of irrepressible horror.

'Let me go!' she said hoarsely. 'I must be alone. Let me go, mother. I cannot bear it!'

'Kiss me before you go,' said Mrs. Clanricarde, who was really frightened.

'Kiss you!' said Estelle. 'No; you are his murderess! I will never kiss you again!'

For the moment she was in truth and in deed absolutely mad.

'Good God! have I gone too far?' thought Mrs. Clanricarde. 'Is her brain really turned?'

With a strange gesture and a face that had

only her features but none of her natural expression, the girl turned from the room and went upstairs to her own, where she double-locked the door and shut herself in with her sorrow and despair. All that day she remained invisible; would not open the door, nor come downstairs; would not eat; would scarcely answer when they knocked—sitting there in a kind of trance wherein her soul went down into the grave. Her mother's prayers went for nothing; she returned only short monosyllables in reply—monosyllables which would have been fierce had they not been so dry and dead. To her father her tone was somewhat softer. He was free from blood-guiltiness, and had not helped in the murder of her beloved. His voice did not irritate her nerves nor penetrate into her wound, nor did it sound as if rejoicing over the death of him who was as Baldur, the Sun-god, or as Adonis was to Venus. She could endure his voice; but her mother's was like poison in her veins and madness to her whole being. At last Mrs. Clanricarde, whose compassion was at all times but a rather shallow stream, tired of this dumb strife and mute rebellion, peremptorily commanded her to open the door and see her and speak to her. And Estelle, overcome by the force of habit, did as she was told, and let her mother enter.

Mrs. Clanricarde gave a little cry when she saw her daughter. From two o'clock until now, ten, she had changed almost as if she had been transformed. All the tender, supple, timid grace had gone out of her face and figure. There was no shyness in her eyes, no love upon her lips, no line of yielding, of sympathy, of girlish love, of womanly softness left in her. She looked like a modern Medusa, turned to stone for her own part, and capable of turning to stone all those who looked on her. No tears were in her eyes, and none had been. Her parted lips were as dry and as pathetic as the Cenci's, but they were less loving. She was as one dead while living; or, if she showed anything at all, it was just so much of the passion of resentment as made her a woman and not a curious bit of vitalized mechanism.

'My dear child! my Estelle!' cried Mrs. Clanricarde, sincerely shocked and stirred.

'What do you want with me, mother?' asked Estelle, coldly.

'Why have you kept away from me?' returned the mother. 'Am I not always here to receive your sorrow and feel with you in your grief?'

'Hush!' said Estelle lifting her hand. 'Not a word of that! *Your* sympathy!' she added with deadly scorn. It had in it the essence of a curse.

Mrs. Clanricarde was morally brave to the point next before insensibility, but even she quivered in all her being at the tone and look with which her daughter repudiated her maternal caress. It was like a bill of divorcement between them.

'I forgive you, Estelle,' she said, trying to speak quietly. 'Your mind is upset, and you are not yourself. You do not know what you say, my poor child, and it is the mother's part to have mercy and to forgive.'

Estelle stood unmoved. All filial feeling

seemed to have died in her—to be submerged in the fiery deluge of her grief for her beloved. Mrs. Clanricarde took her hand, but her daughter shook off her mother's as if it had been some noxious thing that pained her.

'Don't touch me, mother!' she said harshly. 'Leave me to myself. Why have you come to torment me?'

'Now, Estelle, this nonsense must cease,' said Mrs. Clanricarde, suddenly severe in her turn. 'If poor Charlie Osborne has died of fever, is that my fault? Why should you turn against me and behave yourself like a maniac as you are doing? It is absurd, and undutiful as well, and I will not allow it! So I tell you.'

A strange and ominous glare came into those beautiful brown eyes, usually so soft and tender.

'Mother, if you do not leave me at once I shall go mad!' she cried in a hoarse voice that had not a trace of her natural silver, her rightful melody, upon its roughened notes. 'Leave me to myself—that is the only way in which I can live. You send me mad to see and hear you.'

'And you are a wicked, undutiful girl; but I forgive you, and I am always your mother ready to receive and comfort you,' said Mrs. Clanricarde, part revolted, part frightened by this outburst, as she turned and left the room, halting at the door to say: 'At least promise me one thing, Estelle—do not lock your door.'

'If you will promise not to open it,' said Estelle, in the same rough and unnatural tones, making a step forward. On which her mother left her, and the girl went back into the fiery hell of her despair.

'I wish I had never seen you!' cried Mrs. Clanricarde with true French peevishness to that unlucky George. 'Everything connected with you turns ill. Here is now mademoiselle, your daughter, a stark staring lunatic, because that absurd young man has died at Yokohama. From such a father what else can be expected!'

That unlucky George smiled fatuously. Then his eyes filled up with tears. He loved Estelle with more intrinsic tenderness—more simplicity of affection—than did her mother, and he felt for her in her present trial with a faithfulness of sympathy which that mother could not compass nor even understand.

'Poor Estelle!' he said. 'It is a hard trial for her.'

'God sends us all trials,' said Mrs. Clanricarde, with the tart religiosity of the cross-tempered. 'Estelle has to submit, as we all must. I have to endure you,' she added, a little below her breath.

But her husband did not hear. He was great at not hearing, as at times he was great at not seeing. And then sleep came down over the household, and only the miserable Estelle stood by the window, looking up to the starry sky, wondering in which bright point her darling's soul was placed, sure that he was looking down on her and pitying her despair.

'He, at least, is happy,' she said to herself again and again for reassurance. 'I am selfish to be so wretched! I should be happy, knowing that he is out of pain and sorrow. But oh! he would have been so happy had he lived, with my love, as I with his. Oh, that we might have known that love—that dear sweet life together, before God had taken him to Himself.'

It was the cry of the human heart making itself heard in spite of all the comforting assurances of faith—the pitiful sob of love, stronger than death and dearer than the eternal heaven of peace and unfading joy.

CHAPTER XIII.

THE LAYING OF THE GROUND.

DAYS passed, and Estelle was still invisible to the world outside Les Saules, and but rarely to that within. She was ill, her mother said to Anthony Harford and all other inquirers; which indeed was but too true, and ill as much mentally as physically. Something seemed to have snapped in her—something that would never be renewed. She had lost all interest in things, and even in life itself. Her painting, her music, her embroidery—all her pretty girlish work was neglected and laid aside; and she was more like those soulless women of romance—women only by form, not by nature—than a living, loving daughter of man.

She would see no one—not even Lady Elizabeth—and certainly not Anthony Harford. For him, indeed, she showed so much shuddering repugnance that her mother was afraid to press her. Her mother was afraid of her altogether; and constantly pondered within herself on the chances of the poor child's ultimate recovery. But Time—Time—that bale and blessing of the world—Time would do all, and the wound would be healed at last. Life would probably never be the same to her as before; but we have to make up with scraps and fragments when the first fresh wholeness has gone. And she would have to do her duty, willing or unwilling. The sacrifice of herself had to be made, cost her what it would. She had to be Anthony's wife, though she paid the supreme forfeit in return.

On this point Mrs. Clanricarde was inexorable. She was emphatically a modern mother with whom love counts as folly, and money is the only desirable good in marriage—who will welcome as her son-in-law a moral leper or a physical, if sufficiently well gilded—to whom a daughter's heart is merely a muscular arrangement, to be pressed down when inconveniently active and to be ignored when only passively suffering. This phase of modern maternity had commended itself to Mrs. Clanricarde as the most rational and the most duty doing; and Estelle had to submit to her mother's principles, as girls must.

During this time of the girl's first anguish of despair Anthony Harford's state was only a shade less pitiable than hers. All Kingshouse had, of course, seen the announcement of poor Charlie's death, and all Kingshouse understood the meaning of Estelle's indisposition. Naturally Anthony's ear had been bombarded again and again with the unwelcome Q. E. D. of gossip. For a jealous man as he was, arbitrary and resolute, this demonstration was so much torture; but he had not lived with hot-blooded cowboys handy with their shooting irons, and high-toned gamblers ready with their bowie-knives, for nothing. He controlled all outward expression of feeling as rigidly as if he had been a true redskin, and only Lady Elizabeth knew what no one else saw nor suspected. From her, indeed, he had now no concealment. She had taken the place of his second self—his incarnate conscience—his visible thought; and that she suffered in her turn from the burden he laid on her was as well concealed from him as that internal rage of his was hidden from the world at large.

Between her and Mrs. Clanricarde Anthony came to what it was meant should be to him the right measure of things.

' A boy's death has pained her. Poor Charlie Osborne was like her brother. They had been brought up together, and they had really a brother's and sister's affection for each other. She has naturally been shocked at the announcement; so, indeed, have we all. Who would not be—such a dear, good, young fellow as he was! But she is not ill on that account. She is ill from a chill, and has a sore throat and fever. It is only this.'

This was Mrs. Clanricarde's smooth-skinned account of things to Mr. Harford when he pressed her closely, and made her give at least the semblance of a reason for Estelle's persistent invisibility. Lady Elizabeth, however, put matters on a more truthful basis, for indeed she could not be aught but truthful, let the cost be what it might.

'Yes, she was what is meant by "in love" with him,' she said with her gentle straightforwardness when Anthony asked her if there had been anything like a love affair—an engagement—between Miss Clanricarde and this young man, whose name at this moment filled the air; 'and they were in a manner engaged—in that hopeless way where there is no money now and very little chance of any hereafterwards—where the engagement is only between themselves—not known to the world nor sanctioned by the parents.'

'But he is dead now,' said Anthony.

'Poor dear Charlie! yes, too surely!' said Lady Elizabeth.

'And was he such a wonderful person, really now?' asked Anthony, with no unnecessary suavity—with scarcely as much, indeed, as was quite necessary.

'Yes,' said Lady Elizabeth; 'he was a dear fellow.   We all liked him.'

'You, too, Lady Elizabeth?'

'I, too,' she said.

'But he is dead now,' repeated Anthony, a little more harshly than even before.   'And no woman loves the dead for ever, to the exclusion of the living,' he added.

Lady Elizabeth did not answer.   In her own mind she thought it probable that Estelle would go on loving Charlie dead as she had loved him living.   Once to love would be always to love with herself; and she credited her poor, broken-hearted friend with her own constancy.

'She shall forget him,' continued Anthony, in a certain sense piqued by her non-response. 'I will love her so that she shall not remember him, still less lament him.   She shall find her happiness in my arms,' he went on more as if speaking to himself than to a listener.   'She shall be so happy in my love, so well cared for, that she will not even wish to change could her wish bring back the dead.'

Lady Elizabeth's face became as pale as the snowdrops in the vase beside her.

'If she married you I know that you would be good to her,' she said, in a low, level voice, without inflection or emphasis.

'If? She shall!' returned Anthony, speaking with the intensity of constrained passion. 'Neither man nor devil shall keep her from me! She is destined.'

'Hush!' said Lady Elizabeth, blanched to her very lips. 'You make me shudder.'

'Why?' he asked, with all his usual gentleness, all the chivalrous tenderness which was his ordinary bearing when he spoke to her. 'Why should you shudder?'

'It seems almost as if you were forcing fate —compelling your own destiny—which is always sorrow,' she said.

He took both her hands. It was his favourite action with her.

'Oh, you Delight,' he said with a smile. 'Are you, too, daughter of the gods as you are, superstitious like the little people whose brains are no bigger than pigmies'?'

'Who can help it who cares for another's happiness?' was her ingenuous reply, made steadily and without shamefacedness.

'And you care for mine?'

'Yes, indeed,' she answered. She still spoke with steadiness, direct and unashamed.

'How I wish you were my sister!' said Anthony. 'Estelle my wife—you my sister—I would ask nothing more from heaven but long life to enjoy my superb happiness.'

Something, she did not know what it was, nor could she control it, seemed to come up into Lady Elizabeth's eyes and throat. She felt choking, as if deep waters were closing over her head—as if she must cry out for help. Help for what? She could not answer. Her voice had gone; she had no power of speech left in her; but Anthony, irritable and sore on his own side, read nothing of the truth as it was. He thought her silence was from offended pride, and that she resented this intimate bracketing of a life, 'not born,' as the Germans say, when compared with her own.

'Are you offended at such close association?' he asked, all his pride in his voice.

She shook her head and faintly smiled. Then with a supreme effort she conquered her strange emotion and said:

'No, no, indeed not!' steadily.

Anthony looked at her with an odd, perplexed expression in his face. For a moment his deep-set eyes seemed to scrutinize, to ask, to consider. Then it was as if he shook himself clear of something that disturbed and distracted him, and his face took back the frankly confident look it always had when with Lady Elizabeth—and with no one but her.

'I have set all my heart and all my hope on this card,' he said, returning to his main thought. 'I may be euchred, but if I am——'

'You will know how to bear your disappointment bravely,' said Lady Elizabeth, thinking of Caleb.

'Bravely? I do not know about that, from your point of view,' he said. 'From my own, yes, bravely enough.'

'Your point of view is sure to be right,' she answered, not so much in the tone of perfect assurance, as of heartening by that kind of trust which is more exhortation than certainty.

'Thank you,' said Anthony, thinking to himself: 'Would she say this if she knew?'

After some further talk Mr. Harford left the Dower House, no nearer, truly, to his great desire that when he had gone there, but with a heart somewhat lightened, in that vague manner of a clearer moral atmosphere where, though things are not more definite, the clouds seem to have lifted.

During all these days of Estelle's seclusion Anthony Harford was like a soul in pain. Restless, distracted, he inflicted his trouble on his friend, who had to bear his burden as well as her own, and not to show where it galled and pressed. He avoided Hindfleet, but he almost lived at the Dower House, where, however, he did not shine with quite the same brilliancy as in the beginning. Some of the quainter forms of his adopted speech were falling from him, and he was becoming daily more English and less American—reverting to his original condition with natural rapidity. Still, he was racier than most and more unconventional than most, and if not quite so 'hors de ligne,' as in the beginning, quite enough so to interest the earl and amuse the countess; while their daughter accepted the pain, of which she alone herself was conscious, with the sweet steadfastness of a Christian martyr, making no sign.

At last time worked its partial cure so far that Estelle consented to reappear in the world. The sharpness of her anguish, which had for the moment warped her brain and which still dulled her normal affections, had given place to a dull aching and a leaden kind of indifference. It did not much matter now how things went. She had lost the centre of her life's interest— the dear love she had worshipped as a fire worshipper kneels to the sun—and for the rest what did it signify? Something in her had given way, like the snapping of a chain, and her mind did not work nor suffer as before. She was dead in some part of her being, but she

had not the insensibility of death in all. She
was more beautiful than ever. The pathos in
her eyes, like those of a wounded animal, went
straight to the heart of those who saw her.
The deadly pallor of her cheeks enhanced the
burning crimson of her feverish lips; and the
curling rings of raven hair enhanced the white-
ness of her skin. Something had come and
something had gone, but the result was even a
greater charm and more wonderful beauty of
face and mien. Such love as Anthony Harford had already felt, flamed hotter and higher
when he saw her for the first time after her
illness. He would not see in her state the
result of grief, only the result of physical ail-
ment; and he felt for her in consequence that
very passion of tenderness which strong men
feel for the woman they love, when those
women are even more helpless than usual, more
frail and more dependent.

'I am glad to see you again, and sorry you have
been sick,' he said, holding her hand in both of
his.

'Thank you, I am better,' she answered wearily, not looking at him.

'You have been very sick, I can see that,' he continued with great tenderness.

She made no reply. She only drew away her hand, more coldly than with repugnance. A spasm crossed Anthony's face, like a shadow. It was repeated in Mrs. Clanricarde's.

'She will spoil everything,' she thought to herself. 'Was ever mother cursed so as I?'

'You should give her change of air, Mrs. Clanricarde,' said Anthony, turning to the mother.

Mrs. Clanricarde looked out of the window. The rain was falling fast—that cold, harsh rain of the retreating winter flinging its Parthian darts before the spring finally chases it away.

'It is scarcely the weather for the sea,' she said; 'and London air is not bracing.'

She did not add, 'and too costly for my crippled purse,' which she might have done had she been careful for the truth.

'The air at Thrift is notoriously fine,' said

Anthony hastily. 'I must be back there next week. Why not come with me for a change, all three of you? I am sure it would do Miss Clanricarde good in every way.'

He added these last words in the spirit of a woman's postscript—as a rider that included more than the main text.

'That would be delightful!' said Mrs. Clanricarde eagerly. 'I know that change is just what Estelle wants to set her up again. But, unless one went to a friend's house there is more chance of harm than of good from it. Lodgings and hotels are so comfortless! One's own home or a friend's well-appointed house—that is the only thing we can do.'

'Then you will come?' he added. 'Will you like that, Miss Clanricarde? Will you like to come to my place?' he added, speaking directly to Estelle.

'No,' said Estelle, with a sudden look of fear in her eyes. 'Do not go, mother! do not let us leave home!'

'It will do you good, my dear,' answered her mother suavely. 'It is for your own sake.'

'If for mine, then I do not wish it,' persisted the girl.

'It will do you good,' said Anthony.

'I do not want any good done to me,' she answered, with curious sullenness—curious, that is in the girl she used to be; common enough alas! in these later times.

Her opposition wrought the usual effect of all opposition on Anthony. It strengthened his resolve and braced his determination.

'Your mother consents, and I hold her to her promise,' he said with sudden sternness. 'If it is disagreeable to you, you can make tracks home if you like. But you've got to come and see for yourself.'

'Mother!' appealed Estelle.

'Don't be silly, child,' said Mrs. Clanricarde with affected banter and real displeasure. 'What is there to object to in paying a visit to a beautiful country-house in a superb country place? One would think you were asked to go to a prison!'

'You are not very flattering to me either,' said Anthony as sternly as before.

He was not so supple as Mrs. Clanricarde, and he did not think his habitual self-command quite in place at this moment.

'I do not wish to flatter you,' said Estelle drawing herself up, and speaking with intense haughtiness.

Was this really Estelle Clanricarde, that timid, sweet and fawn-like girl whose nature had hitherto been like that of a sensitive-plant, drooping under a touch, influenced even by a breath?

Anthony saw the folly and humiliation of a war of words with a girl in such a mood.

'Well, no,' he laughed with a good-humour as forced as Mrs. Clanricarde's banter had been. 'That would scarcely be the way. At all events we have got so far on the road—so much is settled. You and your father and mother will come with me to Thrift next week, and you will get back there all your roses, I promise you.'

'So far the ground is laid,' said Anthony to himself. 'All now depends on myself.'

CHAPTER XIV.

HER ADVANCING DOOM.

AGAINST that fatal visit to Thrift, which Estelle knew too well would be her doom, she made such resistance as was in her power. She revolted openly at home and silently to Anthony Harford, whom, however, she could not repulse with absolute directness. She had no 'locus standi,' for he gave her none. She could not tell him that she would not marry him, when he had not yet asked her : and her mother, made wise by experience, was careful not to even hint at such a contingency. The whole thing was in the air, voiceless and formless, but none the less there. Estelle knew that she was going to her ruin and despair, but she could not save herself. She was like another Iphigenia, bound in her saffron-coloured garments, and held as a kid above the sacrificial altar. And just as the hapless Greek maiden appealed in vain to her executioners, so did she struggle against hers— against the mother who mutely offered, and against the lover who as mutely accepted, the sacrifice of more than her mere life.

There was no help for her. Charlie was dead; things financial at home were going rapidly from bad to worse; and there was no one to whom she could turn. Sometimes she thought of appealing to Caleb Stagg. Between the two she would rather call him her husband than be Anthony Harford's wife. With the one she would be her own mistress and his queen, honoured and obeyed; with the other she would be a slave, caressed and well cared for, but always a slave. The very unpersonableness of Caleb made him less shameful in her mind; while the superb personality of Anthony seemed to justify her treachery to her dead lover's memory. The most miserable creature be-

tween earth and sky at this moment to be
found in a decent English home was this same
beautiful Estelle Clanricarde—this woman fatal
to men, and therefore the enemy of her own
peace—this woman obsessed and in a manner
destroyed by the excess of that love of which
so many pale, pining sisters have not enough to
keep them alive.

The day before this dreadful visit was to take
place Estelle went alone to the Dower House.
It was the first day that she had gone out since
the fatal announcement of poor Charlie's death,
and she had a sudden desire to see Lady Elizabeth, whom, by the way, she had refused to see
for all these days of mourning. Mrs. Clanricarde
wanted to go with her, but Estelle showed so
much temper at the proposal—how changed
she was from the sweet-natured, pliant, loving
girl of the happier past!—that the mother gave
way. She had all but secured the main thing,
she thought; the minor might go. All the
same, she was a little uneasy. Estelle's state
was strange and strained, and evil thoughts
might possess her disastrously. But she yielded,

and her daughter walked over to the Dower House alone.

The spring was stealing over the earth, and all the first signs and sounds of the renewed love-time of nature were about. The first pale flowers had come as the first young leaves— while the later were still folded up in their shining buds. The twigs and branchlets of the hawthorn were red as with living blood; the birds were singing in the bushes; the air was sweet and fresh. The whole atmosphere was one of love, and Estelle, essentially the child of the country, felt to her inmost being the whole meaning of the day and time, and received into her heart the message given to her by love. But love and death were now one with her; and as she walked, the tears gathered silently into her eyes and fell down her face unheeded. How all these circumstances of the time had once been as messages and words sent by Charlie! And now he was lying in his grave as pale as those snowdrops, as cold as that snowdrift still heaped within the sunless ravine there on the fell. Ah, how sad life was to her now! What a sorrowful funeral chant in place of that once jocund hymn of praise and joy! Then she thought of Anthony Harford, and the funeral chant changed to a still deeper threnody, which made her shiver as if in a fever fit.

She found Lady Elizabeth at home, and the two friends met, as they had parted, in all confidence and affection, all trust and love, though only one of the two knew the whole truth of their joint position. And even she did not know the whole truth all round. Each was frankly shocked at the change which these few weeks had wrought in the other. Each was like a faded photograph of the past. But where Lady Elizabeth had, as it were, sublimed into a more etherealized self—a self which had come out of a spiritual conflict the victor at a cost of physical vitality—Estelle had chilled and hardened, as something which had become petrified rather than etherealized.

'Oh, Liese, I am so miserable!' cried Estelle, as she clung to her friend.

It was the most human and the most natural

thing she had said since that deadly night.

'Darling, you must be!' returned Lady Elizabeth, holding her in her arms and kissing her as a young mother would kiss her sorrowing child.

'And as if I had not enough to bear, there is now this hateful man!' said Estelle, with the strange vehemence which sometimes possessed her of late—vehemence traversing her deadness like lightning piercing a thundercloud.

Lady Elizabeth checked the sudden quiver that came over her. She did not answer. She only pressed the poor girl yet more tenderly to her heart. Free from all the littleness of jealousy as she was, she loved Estelle the more because Anthony Harford loved her, and would, if she could, have made her love him in return. If she could not make his happiness herself she did not hate the one who could; nor did she wish his to be incomplete through the want of that other's love. But to call Anthony Harford 'that hateful man,' hurt her ears as blasphemy in its own way.

'I daresay you think me vain and horrid,'

continued Estelle, 'for speaking of him as if I had the right to hate him. But we all know those things too well; we know when men are in love with us and mean to make an offer. And then there is my mother—and Liese! Liese! between them both I am lost! I sometimes think I will kill myself, and so have done with the whole thing. Now that Charlie is gone, why should I live?'

'Hush, darling!' said Lady Elizabeth gently. 'I cannot hear such things even from you. You must not even think them, dear, still less say them.'

'Why should I live?' she repeated sullenly, yet despairingly. 'To be made the loathing wife of a man I hate! I know that mother will force me into it. If it broke my heart she would not mind, so long as I married a rich man.'

'But if he sees your dislike,' said Lady Elizabeth tentatively.

'Oh! what would he care for that?' answered Estelle disdainfully. 'He does see it—he knows it well enough! I make him feel it, and have done so almost from the first; but he is just one of those selfish, self-willed savages who care only for themselves. He does not mind whether I hate him or not, so long as he gets his own way!'

'You are a little hard on him, dear,' said Lady Elizabeth, always gently. 'You see, when people are in love—they are—and they cannot help themselves.'

Her argument was more natural than convincing or logical, but it served her turn.

'But if you are not in love with them they ought to get over it,' said Estelle loftily. 'That poor Caleb Stagg did, and so ought this man. He would, if he were good or a real gentleman.'

'You do hate him!' cried Lady Elizabeth with an accent of surprise in her voice.

'I do!' answered Estelle emphatically; 'and I always shall.'

'But if you have to marry him?' asked her friend, full of compassion for both—for the man who loved in vain, for the woman who had to yield to a love she neither shared nor desired.

'I will not marry him!' said Estelle, vehemently. 'I will say "No" before the altar!'

Alas! alas! these passionate words were but the struggles of the victim—the beating of the caged bird's wings against the cruel bars. Deep down in her own heart she knew that her mother's will would overpower hers. Lady Elizabeth knew so too.

'Oh, help me, Liese!' cried this poor uncelebrated Iphigenia, burying her face on her friend's knees as she flung herself to the ground and clasped that flexible waist with her trembling hands.

'How can I, dear? how can I?' said Lady Elizabeth, in a kind of agony.

'Make him in love with you,' said Estelle—as she might have said, 'Give me wings to fly away and be at rest.' 'You are so much better a match than I am in every way. Why did he not fall in love with you from the first? It would be so easy to make him, now!'

For a few seconds Lady Elizabeth did not speak. The demands made by friendship on one's patience, one's endurance, are sometimes

very hard, and duty is oftener rude than sweet.
But she had to speak; and to speak so that Estelle should not understand.

'Do you think hearts are like shuttlecocks,
dear?' she asked gently. 'If Mr. Harford
loves you what can he see in me? and how could
I, even for you, play such a mean part as to try
to make a man in love with me when he is not
so of his own free will? Besides, I could not if
I did try.'

'Then tell him how much I hate him,' cried
Estelle.

'And how can I do even that, dear?' her friend
again remonstrated. 'He has not yet said that
he loves you. How can I, with any regard to
your dignity, tell him this?'

'Yes, you can!' said Estelle almost fiercely.
'And if you loved me, Liese, you would!'

'I do love you, darling—you know I do; but
I could not say this to Mr. Harford. It is the
kind of thing that only the person's own self can
say.'

'And I will!' said Estelle, still in that same
fierce and unnatural way by which she was, as

it were, transformed from her real self and made into another creature. As indeed she was. Her grief had just a little warped her brain and darkened the mild radiance of her moral nature. Had there not been this additional distress of an unwelcome admirer she would have suffered as keenly but with less bitterness. And she would have worked round to her normal condition in due time, when she had forded the Jordan of her sorrow. But Anthony Harford and her mother were the real drops of bitterness in her cup, and it was they who had poisoned the arrow of death so that the wound festered into almost madness.

'If I am made to marry him I will kill myself!' she then said after a pause. 'I feel as sure as of my own existence that he intends to ask me when we are at his horrible place, and that mother means to force me to accept him. That is why we are going! I feel it. I know it. And I will not! I should be wicked and false to myself if I did. I should always feel my poor dear dead darling's wife. I should never feel really and rightly married to this hateful man.

And how can I marry, feeling as I do ?   It would be a crime !   Do feelings count for nothing ? Why, they are everything !   Tell me, Liese ; how could I ?'

Lady Elizabeth did not answer.   What could she say ?   It was not for her to dissuade another woman—and the woman he loved—from making the happiness of a man as dear to her as Anthony Harford ; nor was it for her, as a woman, to persuade a sister to forswear herself, and give her body without her heart, herself without her love.   She was, as it were, caught between two fires, and she had to suffer from the scorching of each.   And just for one moment she thought that her own place was almost as hard as Estelle's, and that there are other deaths beside that of the body, as we know it.

At this moment the door-bell rang, and Mr. Harford was brought up into Lady Elizabeth's sanctuary, where the two girls were.   Lady Kingshouse was never visible before luncheon. My Lord was in bed after a protracted 'sweep' last night ; and only Lady Elizabeth was available—as Anthony knew.   He had been sent on

here by Mrs. Clanricarde. He had called at Les
Saules, and she, glad of his escort and protection
from herself for Estelle, told him where she was
to be found, and suggested his going to find her
and bring her home. Which suggestion he had
adopted gladly enough. When he entered the
room something came over her friend's face
which startled Estelle, preoccupied as she was
with her own troubles. Pale as Lady Elizabeth
was before, she became paler still; and her calm
dignity of manner had a certain strained and
almost unnatural stillness, as if she were forcing
herself to be unexpressive. Indeed, it was
glacial rather than merely calm, as is the way
with those who have something to hide. But
though Estelle saw she did not understand.
She had none of that sharpness of perception
which makes the born detective. What passed
before her eyes passed unfathomed—this change
in Lady Elizbeth's manner and her greater
pallor among the rest. It was only afterwards,
when still further enlightened by her own
sufferings, that she remembered what she had
seen, and then she read the underneath of the

cards. At the moment she took it to be a kind of consciousness of their conversation, such as sensitive people have when they have talked of things they would not wish the newcomer to hear.

Very soon after Anthony came in Estelle rose to go. Anthony, who had not even sat down, made a step forward as if to go too.

'Are you going?' he asked in his quiet masterful way.

'Yes,' said Estelle hurriedly.

'Good-bye, Lady Elizabeth,' said Anthony.

'You need not come, Mr. Harford,' exclaimed Estelle.

'Yes, I have got to take you home,' he answered.

'I do not want you,' said Estelle, turning from him abruptly, and speaking as abruptly as had been her action.

'That is not the question,' he laughed a little grimly. 'Your mamma'—he pronounced it 'marmar'—'told me I was to take you back. So here I am.'

' I would rather you did not,' said Estelle, her colour rising and her dark eyes growing gloomy beneath her lowered brow.

' I have got to,' was the reply, made without the smallest show of feeling, certainly with none of yielding.

He stood as if on parade, erect, determined, inflexible ; and Estelle felt that to try and deflect that stubborn will was like trying to soften granite with her tears—to move the eternal rock by her prayers.

' I think it very unkind of you, Mr. Harford— very ungentlemanlike to do what I don't wish,' she cried, flashing out into one of the strange tempers which, since the announcement of Charlie's death, had been all too familiar and frequent with her.

Anthony's bronze cheeks grew livid.

' I am sorry if you are displeased,' he said, just as quiet as usual in tone and manner, but with an ominous flash in his eyes to match the gloomy anger in hers ; ' but I have your mamma's orders and I must obey them. I have got to take you home.'

'Then I shall not go at all. I shall stay here,' said Estelle.

'As you like,' answered Anthony, seating himself.

Estelle burst into tears. They were tears of wounded pride, of annoyance only, and did nothing to dissolve that terrible hardness—to damp down that consuming fire in her veins.

'I am sorry to be so distasteful an escort,' said Anthony; but if he was sorry, his sorrow was very like sternness. 'You have got to submit, however, and you have to let me walk with you home.'

'I wish I was dead,' said Estelle passionately.

'It's but a little matter to raise Cain for,' said Anthony drily.

All this time Lady Elizabeth had not spoken. She had not been appealed to by either, and she would have been hard put to it if she had. She too felt that Estelle in her present mood was best accompanied, and that even Anthony's ungracious persistence had its valuable side.

'I would go with you, dear,' she said in a low

voice; 'but I have promised my father to ride with him after luncheon; and it is close on luncheon time now.'

'Come, Miss Clanricarde. It is time we were going,' said Anthony who had overheard her. 'I promised to take you back for lunch.'

There was nothing for it but to obey. She was caught and caged here too, as in other things and at other times. Anthony said she had got to do it, and she could not help herself. But she resolved to make that walk back to Les Saules as unpleasant as she knew how; and Anthony wished twenty times before it was over that his pride would let him mount his horse and ride away from her as from one whose dismissal he understood and accepted. He suffered as she meant he should. But it was to no good. Her very reluctance acted as a spur, not a check. She enraged him, but she strengthened his resolve by that very rage. He had sworn that he would marry her, and he meant to do as he had sworn. Her sick fancies and girlish impertinence should not deter him. When she was all his own things would come right. He trusted to his own power then to win her. No woman that he loved could resist him, he thought in the plenitude of his self-confidence—his pride. And he loved her so violently, so passionately, he must, by the very logic of things—the very law of sequence and cause and effect—make her love him when once he had the right to lavish all the treasures of his heart upon her. So he reasoned and so he thought within himself, while he walked by Estelle's side, leading his horse and talking to her as easily as if she loved the sound of his voice and enjoyed his anecdotes instead of hating them—enjoyed them as much say as Lady Elizabeth would have done. Then her dreary penance accomplished, they reached home at last; when Anthony's horse was put up in the stable and he himself was asked to stay for luncheon and through the afternoon. And Estelle was not suffered by her mother to escape upstairs into solitude as she wished; and by that mother's presence and authority was forced into some faint show of politeness to their guest—politeness, perhaps, but certainly not amiability.

The next day they all left Les Saules; and when the evening came they were seated at Anthony's own table at Thrift by Thorbergh—where Mrs. Latimer and Mary Crosby lived.

CHAPTER XV.

THE SETTING-IN OF THE NIGHT.

How often since the time of Tacitus has that desert made by oppression been called Peace! When the creature is dead the struggle is over and the victory is secure. But the creature is dead all the same. Still, if beautiful, there is always its skin, which art can make to look passably alive. It was so now. The thing was done; the end was gained. The dreaded offer was finally made; and, if not accepted in any sense of graciousness, it was assented to as perforce. What can the wildest hawk that ever flew across the mountain tops into space do when hooded and held? It must sit quiet on the hand that holds it. It cannot see and it cannot fly. Nor could Estelle resist. It had been a hard fight, but the authorities had conquered; and they had killed her essential being in the victory. This was an accident that did not count. What they had fought for they had won, and the mischances of the war were integral to the account. They must be accepted, however severe they might be.

Things financial had grown worse and ever worse at home, and had now come to their climax. This failure and that had still further contracted the meagre capital left undissolved by the acids of former failures; and now Mr. Clanricarde would be declared bankrupt unless help should come from the skies. Saving this miracle it could come to him only through Estelle's marriage. On the wedding-day Mr. Harford promised to hand over to his father-in-law such and such sums as should release him from his troubles, and set him square before the world and with his creditors. But only on his wedding-day. The English gentleman had learned so much of diplomatic caution and astute reserve from his American experiences as to make his promise contingent, not absolute. When Estelle's hand was in his, the money should be her father's. Then, without fail—but not an hour before.

' Would a daughter allow this terrible ruin to fall on the honoured heads of her beloved and loving parents, that she might indulge her very proper and natural grief unchecked ? Would not such indulgence be selfish—sacred as her grief might be ?'

Mrs. Clanricarde was careful of her adjectives, and specially solicitous to speak of Estelle's sorrow with becoming respect. It was no longer a 'foolish fancy,' not worth a second thought. It had been a serious and honourable love, the light of which was now quenched in the grave of a respectable sorrow. But this sorrow had to be in its turn overcome for a noble purpose—one nobler than mere verbal fidelity.

The mother touched the daughter's heart by her reasoning, her sympathy, her manner. She made her weep as she had not wept since Charlie's death, when she herself, that mother, honestly moved—for, indeed, the peril was great!—earnestly, almost humbly besought her child for this sacrifice of self to save her and her father. That father, too, at last dismayed, and as destitute of hope as of assets, added his prayers to his wife's; and Estelle was at once softened into pity and trained into the strength of sacrifice. She would immolate herself for their gain. Out of the ashes of her own happiness should rise their safety; and Charlie in heaven would see and understand—and, therefore, he would not only forgive but would bless this seeming perfidy. He would know why, and he would read her heart. He would know that never for one instant had her thoughts, her love, her faithfulness strayed from him ; and that this gift of her poor person was but the bestowal of the husk, the shell, the mask, while all the time the life and the core were in his grave for ever.

So she thought, her beautiful brown eyes raised to the cloud-flecked sky, as if trying to see her lover's glorified form somewhere like a cloud itself against the blue; and then, with the passionate sense of sacrifice for duty's sake, she turned to her father and mother, and in a low, soft, solemn voice, said : ' Yes ; let it be so !'

'And God will bless you now and for ever !' said Mrs. Clanricarde, taking her in her arms and weeping genuine tears of both sympathy and relief. The relief, indeed, suffered the sympathy to exist. Now that she had no longer her own anxieties to think of she could spare thought for her daughter's sufferings. And, while she accepted, she realized the magnitude of the sacrifice she had urged. But the father, who had always been the most sympathetic of the two, was now the least. The peril of the moment had swamped all other considerations, and he had the irresistible selfishness of a weak nature not strong enough for altruism.

With a hurried kiss, that somewhat hurt Estelle more than if it had been a sharp word, he slipped from the room and went to Anthony, waiting in the library. The strong man had been forced to fight under cover. That fair fortress would not yield to him. He knew that well enough. He had to negotiate through other media, and to employ all such agents as he could press into his service. The result proved his wisdom. To himself, unsupported by those passionate prayers of her mother, Estelle would never have yielded. For that mother's sake she did; and Anthony set his teeth over the method and accepted what it brought him without too great mental discomfort.

She was his now, and he had won the day, while she had nothing for it but to accept things as they came. She had to submit to his grave caress, in which was a tumult of passion she neither saw nor dreamed of. She was his victim and his captive, truly; but he would make her his willing slave while he treated her as his sceptred queen. All the tenderness that man can show to woman he poured out on her now, as he ever would; and in time—in time so short as to be a mere nothing—he would win her to himself for ever and ever. No knight of olden time was ever more loyally devoted than was

Anthony Harford to this beautiful Elle woman, whose body was empty of its heart and soul. No lover of old romance was ever more tender, more assiduous. He seemed but to live in her eyes—but to live for her happiness. All that he did was so grave and tender, so full of knightly courtesy and devotion, that Estelle herself was almost touched to pity the passion she loathed rather than shared. But she herself was in a state of exaltation as unreal as all the rest. She knew that she was going to her martyrdom; but she was like a Hindu widow made insensible to pain and dead to reality by the intoxication of spiritual belief. She scarcely felt her position as it was. She was giving herself for her parents, and she did not look too narrowly at the method of her sacrifice. All she knew was that she was engaged to marry Anthony Harford; that the engagement was publicly announced; that her marriage would free her parents from ruin; and that Charlie Osborne was lying dead in his grave beneath the far-off skies of Japan.

The news spread like wild-fire over dry grass

when it reached the loose-hung tongues of
Kingshouse. Everybody fell foul of Mrs. Clanricarde as a 'managing mother,' a 'match-
maker,' and all the rest of it. They fell foul
of her, not knowing how much cause lay behind—only Lady Elizabeth and Caleb Stagg
being able to measure the amount of pressure
that must have been put on the poor girl to
bring her to this pass. For the rest it was
simply the curious kind of envy which pos-
sesses people when they see the success of a
comrade, even when that success takes nothing
from themselves. Mrs. Aspline did not want
Anthony for herself nor for Anne; nor did Anne,
on her own account. Still, these two were the
most bitter at home and most chilly abroad,
when the engagement was discussed—even
anger not tempting that clever Cookey to break
through the rules of careful speech with anything stronger than the damnation of faint
praise, and rigid abstinence from hard words even
when most irate.

Meanwhile, Mr. and Mrs. Clanricarde, with
Anthony and Estelle, called to see Mrs. Latimer.

This was only what was due to the widow of a cousin who had left a tidy little income to his unlucky relation—for all the fact of the mésalliance, which Mrs. Clanricarde's pride could never forgive. They called so far in vain. They could not see the tough old annuitant; for she was ill in bed with the bronchitis, said the tall, well got-up servant, whom Estelle at all events at once recognized as Crosby, Charlie's old nurse, when they were boy and girl together. Her heart went out to this hard-featured resolute-looking woman, as if she had been some part of Charlie's self. So she was, in the spiritual past. She went up to her and laid her hand on her arm.

'Mary!' she said. 'Mary Crosby!'

'Yes, miss; and you are Miss Clanricarde,' returned Mary, the colour coming into her face.

When the party had entered she had been very pale; anxiously erect like a soldier on duty; with an air of resoluteness that was next thing to aggression, and that made her look prepared for a fight.

'I knew you all directly you came in, but I

did not know that you would remember me,' she added more naturally.

'I thought I knew your face,' said Mrs. Clanricarde; 'then you still live with Mrs. Latimer?'

'Yes, ma'am,' said Mary.

'And she is ill to-day?'

'Yes, ma'am. She has the bronchitis. She often has,' replied Mrs. Latimer's faithful attendant.

'Can we not see her?' asked Mrs. Clanricarde.

'I doubt not, ma'am,' said Mary.

'Is she in bed?'

'Yes, in bed upstairs.'

'Have you a doctor?' then put in George.

'I have not sent for him yet, but I shall if Mrs. Latimer gets worse,' said Mary. 'You see, she has the bronchitis so often that I know what to do—with poultices and Dover's powders. The doctor he taught me; so we do not have him for every little bout.'

'I should like to see her,' said George.

'Perhaps she will be better in a day or two,' added Mrs. Clanricarde.

'Perhaps so, ma'am,' said Mary.

'If she wants anything done for her comfort——' said Anthony, leaving the rest to her imagination.

Mary made a curtsey.

'Thank you, sir,' she answered; 'but Mrs. Latimer is a very quiet old lady and gives no trouble to no one.'

'Yes, she is a model tenant,' returned Anthony with a smile.

All this time Estelle had kept close to Mary, looking at her with eyes which love and memory made yet more pathetic than usual. The old wounds opened and bled afresh; the old love rose up like dead Lazarus, from the tomb; and when Anthony touched her arm, and said to her with the lover's voice she had learned to hear without wincing: 'Look here, darling, what a beautiful bit of workmanship this is,'—taking up a Spanish silver-handled knife—she shuddered from head to foot, and involuntarily shrunk as if she had been touched by something noxious. Mary's quick eyes saw the action, as her ears, sharpened to hear all things that might touch her own life, caught the word and tone of lover-like familiarity. She put two and two together in her rapid way; then said suddenly:

'Excuse the liberty, ma'am, but I was that grieved to see the death of poor Master Charlie in the paper.' Here genuine tears came into her eyes. 'I had lost sight of him, but I never forgot him.'

Estelle's face told her all she wanted to know. If her face had not told her, the spasmodic grasp of her arm would have been revelation enough. The poor child turned away from them all, and her thought shaped itself into the one wild prayer that went up like a stifled sob: 'O God, let me die!'

'Yes, poor fellow, it was an awful death, so sudden and unexpected,' said Mrs. Clanricarde; while Anthony's brow grew as black as night, and his dark eyes flashed ominously with sullen fire.

'Come,' he said haughtily to his party; 'we must be going. We evidently shall not see Mrs. Latimer to-day, and time is passing. Good-morning, woman,' to Mary. 'Come, Estelle, let me take you.'

'Good-bye, dear Mary,' said Estelle; and in the face of them all—in defiance of Anthony and of the usual formalities of society—she bent forward and kissed the lips of her dead lover's old nurse, whose eyes had filled with tears when she spoke of his death.

'How unlucky!' said Mrs. Clanricarde to herself, feeling so like Sisyphus!

The stone she had so laboriously rolled to the top had come down again with a thud, and some of the work had to be done over again. But it could not be helped, and the main thing was always secure. Estelle was bound; and Anthony, who knew something if not all, was not indisposed to receive the sacrifice. But he was evidently desperately annoyed, and he made his annoyance felt during the whole of the drive home and for all the evening after.

Meanwhile, Mary felt as one to whom a new vista in a dangerous path has opened itself. She did not clearly see her way, but she knew there was a way which she should some day see, and that it was one which would help her. Estelle Clanricarde was engaged to Mr. Harford, but she had been in love with Master Charlie, and she loved him yet. What could she weave out of that? Who knows? Something was sure to come, 'else,' as she said to Mrs. Latimer, to whom she told all that had passed, 'never call me Mary again.'

The forfeit was not a very tremendous one, but it seemed to carry conviction to both the old lady and her servant; the former saying: 'Lord, Mary, but they did give me a turn;' the latter replying: 'You see you was ill, Mrs. Latimer, and when a body is sick one is apt to have turns.'

At which Mrs. Latimer laughed—for an aged lady with bronchitis it was a good ringing laugh —and said, as she so often said :

'My word, Mary, but you are a brave 'un—as bold as you please, you are !'

'One of us has got to be brave and bold,' said Mary; 'and if it isn't you, Mrs. Latimer, it's bound to be me. And it's very well it is me, all things considered.'

'I hope it may end so,' said Mrs. Latimer a little drily.

CHAPTER XVI.

FRIENDS IN AFFLICTION.

ALL things come in their turn, and the dreaded days are as certain as the desired. Slowly, slowly, but oh! how surely, the day of her doom stole on, coming ever nearer till at last it was there—and poor Estelle had to undergo the pain of her sacrifice with as much courage as she could command. All this time her mother had been indefatigable. She had never suffered that spiritual intoxication to wholly pass away, and it had been hard work to keep it up. The meeting with Mary Crosby had re-opened old wounds truly, but the fact had been turned to the advantage of the moment by the astute diplomatist who could

make all things look as she would have them.
Even the melancholy fact of Charlie's indubit-
able death was skilfully used to enforce the
pressing claims of the living. Anyhow, the
wedding-day came and passed unhindered.

At two o'clock the fatal cortège set out for
the church where Estelle Clanricarde and
Anthony Harford were to be made one bone
and one flesh; and the service was read and the
names were signed without the opposition of
living friend or dead lover. That 'knot had
been tied with the tongue which could not be
undone by the teeth,' and Mrs. Clanricarde
breathed freely once more when the cheque
was placed in their hands which was the price
for their daughter's. The task had been
arduous, the up-hill climb steep and heavy; but
it was done now, and that place of 'rest and be
thankful' had been reached. The tears she
shed over her daughter were tears from mingled
sources. In part they were from pity, and in
part from that terrible exhaustion, that sense of
reaction, which comes after a strain; but Estelle
thought them purely from pity, and loved her

mother with a strange and sudden influx of filial passion for the tenderness she accepted as genuine.

The marriage was entirely private. Lady Elizabeth was away, and could not break her visit to come back even for Estelle and that bridesmaidship which was pressed upon her; and, this being so, Anthony dispensed with the perfunctory services of a 'best man.' They went just as they were—the four immediately concerned; and there was not a vestige of either wedding finery or wedding festivity about the whole affair. They had luncheon before they went, and they all drove together in the 'Kingshouse Arms' close carriage. Estelle wore her travelling dress, which was something as near to black as she could get—a blue as dark as that which 'Bokhara's maids' wear in memory of their loved and lost; and Mrs. Clanricarde was in her ordinary attire. Even the trousseau had not been got, for the day had been hurried on as much as possible; and the minor details were yet to be filled in. What was wanted by the three who had the matter more immediately at heart was speed in completion. The rest was valueless.

The whole thing passed without a hitch of any kind—but one little incident seemed to savour somewhat of mystery. Just before luncheon the post-bag came in. Estelle had long given up her private inspection. There was no use in looking for letters from the grave! To-day, however, her mother, searching the contents, for a brief instant held one in her hand and looked at her daughter. Her look and attitude meant plainly: 'Estelle, here is a letter for you.' With another glance at the envelope she laid it down among her own, and drew a sudden breath as if a danger had been passed. Estelle, a little sullenly knitting, as if uninterested in the day and its event, did not see the look nor catch the half-proffered action of the hand. Neither did she see the look that passed between her father and mother as Mrs. Clanricarde rather hastily unfolded the *Times* and scanned the 'dead and alive' with a certain feverish hurry. Neither, again, did she notice how her mother took the supplement out of the room; nor did it in any way affect her with a sense of strangeness or of mystery that when Anthony came in, he and that mother had one rapid whispered word together. If she had heard it, her life would have been different. That word was from him: 'That damned fellow is alive!'—from her: 'She does not know it, and never must.'

With this exception, the whole running was smooth, and the silken cord without a knot or a kink—that silken cord which to Estelle was the hangman's noose, and which Anthony intended should be as the golden chain that in olden times linked heaven with earth.

After the marriage but little was heard of the bride and bridegroom. Anthony was never an expansive correspondent, and Estelle wrote only once to her mother—a mere address-card in essential meaning, saying they were at Paris, at such and such an hotel, and that the weather was cold and windy. After this no more letters came, and Mrs. Clanricarde was not anxious to hear. She thought it best that the young people should settle down together with the least intervention of outsiders possible; and as she knew that Anthony would be goodness incarnate to his mournful wife, she had no fear on the head of ill-treatment. Her only fears, indeed, were for him, not for Estelle. She was by no means sure that the real trouble of her life might not come from herself—that she might not destroy her chances of happiness by showing her husband too plainly that she did not expect him to make it. Let that be as it would, Mrs. Clanricarde had now nothing on her hands, if still a little on her mind; and if Estelle chose to be that most stupid of all people, a recalcitrant prisoner, that was her own affair, and she alone would suffer. Meanwhile, she read Charlie Osborne's letter—which then she burned —saying to herself she hoped these two would never meet; and—rather weakly for Mrs. Clanricarde, a woman who knew life and could calculate probabilities—she hoped Estelle would never hear that he was alive. And yet, that did not seem very likely in view of the love people have for telling all they know, and proclaiming unpleasant news through trumpets, not to say microphones.

Months passed, and all things at Kingshouse remained pretty much as they were before. There was a certain undefined sadness about Lady Elizabeth which everyone saw and no one understood; and the poor omadhaun had a woebegone look which irritated his father almost to madness, and rendered the one ten times more unpersonable and the other ten times more unbearable than before. Such feeble light as had ever shone on Caleb's unlucky life was quenched as it seemed for ever, and his days had sunk back into yet deeper blackness than erstwhile. His temporary adoption into society had come to an end; and no one now, save Lady Elizabeth and the Stewarts, remembered that he had once been one of themselves—if always a rank outsider, yet still in the running. As for Mrs. Clanricarde, she cut him dead with supreme indifference to all the facts of the past; and had a stranger asked her who that extraordinary-looking individual was, the chances are she would have put up her eye-glass and said: 'I have not an idea!'

Caleb cared little enough for that, save that he was thereby cut off from hearing of Estelle from headquarters. But his was a nature which satisfies itself by thoughts quite as much as by events; and he nursed his love as a poem he was never tired of repeating to himself. It gave him such pleasure as comes from the music of lovely words. For, indeed, if we think of it, the joy of love comes from loving, not from being beloved; and where love is large and selfishness small, there we have the power of such divine abstraction as Caleb knew—with whom thought made happiness, and to love across space was as pure a delight as to have loved in time and presence would have been.

But if Caleb saw but little of some of those who, for a brief hour in the day, had 'taken him up,' and nothing at all of others, he and Lady Elizabeth drew closer and ever closer together. It was a queer choice that she had made of a companion, said the neighbourhood disdainfully. And was she going to take the

young man for good and all? If not, she was
doing him an ill-turn by her kindness, which of
course he would misconstrue. And, even if he
did not, it would set him up too high beyond
his natural deserts and inherited station—of all
offences that which a country society forgives
least. Their sniffs and disdains had but little
weight with either Lady Elizabeth or Caleb—
who, by the way, did not know of them. Perhaps if he had, sensitive and modest as he was,
he would have shrunk back from the lady's
kindness, and have borne his own burden alone.
But she would not have it so. She herself
sought him out, feeling the strangest and most
inexplicable kind of sympathy with him—
a sympathy beyond what she had with any
other person in the place. She seemed to
understand him better than she had ever done,
and to have touched a deeper and still deeper
stratum of his nature. His presence, queer as
it was, soothed her. His beautiful nature,
harnessed to such an unlovely personality, was
like a sonnet of Shakspere's, badly printed and
worse bound. The sonnet was there, and the

divine words breathed and burned through all the raggedness of type and the inferior boards of the cover—but the type was truly ragged and the boards were defaced, and the careless passer-by would not have given a second thought to the book, nor sixpence for its purchase.

One day these oddly-assorted people were walking in the lane which led to Les Saules and the sacred wood of poor Estelle's now unlawful shrine. Lady Elizabeth was on horseback, and Caleb, with his butterfly-net and specimen-box, was walking by her horse. They had been talking of everything but the subject uppermost in the mind of each, till they came to the gate of the picturesque house, now despoiled of its greatest charm.

'I hope she is happy, Lady Elizabeth,' said Caleb suddenly. 'I doubt it; but I hope it.'

'Mr. Harford will do his best,' returned the lady.

'Ay, but it is difficult when the love has all gone another way,' said Caleb. 'And it had all gone with her. I doubt if ever she can call it back.'

'Poor Estelle!' sighed his companion.

Mingled with her pity was a curious kind of wonder how she could be unhappy with Anthony Harford to love her, to care for her, to live with and never more be parted from. And he so far superior to poor dear Charlie Osborne in every way! It was strange. It was too strange for Lady Elizabeth to reconcile with her ideas of right assignment in any way.

'It was a queer thing, that announcement of Mr. Osborne's death,' then said Caleb. 'I have often wondered who was to blame for it. Could it have been Mrs. Clanricarde, think you, Lady Elizabeth?'

'I scarcely like to believe it,' she answered.

'It looks like it,' he repeated.

'I think she wished the marriage very much,' then said Lady Elizabeth. 'Their affairs were in a deplorable state.'

'Ay,' said Caleb simply. 'She would have given that beautiful queen to the least and lowest for a fine ransom. But I doubt if any money will make up to her for what she wanted and had lost.'

' Still, Mr. Harford will be good to her,' said the lady. ' If anyone could make her happy he will.'

' Could anyone but the one she fancied ?' said Caleb.

Enlightened by his own heart he read hers with more accuracy than his generalized knowledge of the world would have given him.

' I suppose not,' said Lady Elizabeth. ' I wish I could believe otherwise !'

At this moment, walking moodily along the lane from the wood where he had been visiting the old places of meeting—graves now of dead joys—they came face to face with Charlie Osborne, looking in his own person more like a ghost than a living man. Pale, lean, cadaverous, his handsome face and graceful figure were like dusky shadows of his former self. He had loved his faithless Star with all his heart and soul. He had rested on her love and faith as a man might rest on a rock; and, lo ! she had failed him. And by her failure the whole world had, as it were, slipped from him. Pare off all that made him human and not heroic—take away his pride and vanity, and that selfishness which is the inseparable companion of weakness—still the residuum showed a true and passionate love for Estelle herself, irrespective of the personal gain and glory of its return. And her desertion and treachery touched him deeply and wounded him to the quick. He alternated between rage and regret—anger and bewailings. Had he not been a man he would have railed like a woman and sobbed like a child. As it was, his large, dark, hollow eyes were suspiciously bright as he met his former rival and Estelle's chief friend, and had not the lane been so narrow that escape was impossible, he would have turned aside rather than have endured the ordeal before him.

'You here!' cried Lady Elizabeth, with more than ordinary kindness of tone and bearing. She had none of that cold manner with which some old friends meet an unexpected visitor—a manner as unmoved as if they had met yesterday, and there was nothing either pleasant or stirring in the encounter. 'When did you come?'

'Last evening,' said Charlie.

'Why did you not come to see us?' she asked again. 'You know my habits. I am always at home in the morning, and I should have been so glad to see you.'

'I have come for only a few hours,' said Charlie a little sullenly. 'I thought I should like to see the old place once more, perhaps for the last time. I did not care to inflict myself on my friends.'

'Charlie! inflict!' she remonstrated.

'Well, perhaps the word is ungracious—at least to you, dear Lady Elizabeth,' he answered with a little tremulousness.

'To all who know you, Mr. Osborne,' put in poor faithful Caleb, though Charlie had not taken the trouble yet to acknowledge him, even by a look. But he bore the impertinence meekly, and put in his gentle word for Estelle's dear sake. The man she loved must be in a way precious to him, and in honouring Charlie

Osborne beyond his deserts he felt that he honoured her, though less than hers.

'Thank you,' said Charlie, recognizing the meaning of this rather clumsily-put compliment. 'Are you all well at Redhill, Mr. Stagg?'

'Yes, thank you, Mr. Osborne,' was the answer. 'Father enjoys good health at times, but mother gets weakly fits at times.'

'And yourself?' he asked.

'Oh, I am always well. I never ail anything,' replied Caleb.

He had become more and more provincial since his practical exclusion from society, when his rough edges were no longer smoothed away by contact with better breeding.

'When will you come to the Dower House?' asked Lady Elizabeth.

'I am afraid not at all,' he answered. 'I am going back to London to-night. I want to find out though,' he added suddenly, 'who put that lying announcement of my death into the *Times*. Was it Mrs. Clanricarde or Mr. Harford?'

He pronounced the hated name with a certain effort as if it would have choked him.

'No one knows who it was,' said Lady Elizabeth. 'But I am sure it was not Mr. Harford,' she added with emphasis. 'He is not the kind of man to do such a thing as that.'

'If it was the mother——' began Charlie. He did not complete his sentence nor say what would follow that contingency. 'I telegraphed the contradiction as soon as I saw it,' he continued. 'It was in the papers on the twenty-sixth of April.'

'Yes,' she answered.

'And there ought to have been a letter from me on the same day,' he continued. 'As soon as I was able I wrote to her to tell her that I had been ill, but was recovering. She should have got it on the twenty-sixth, for I kept note of time and dates.'

'I do not suppose she was allowed to have that. And perhaps it was better as things were,' said Lady Elizabeth.

'Not better,' he answered fiercely; 'if it had prevented this hideous sacrilege. I am sure she would not have committed this crime if she had known that I was alive!'

This was one of his thoughts. Another was that she had voluntarily sold herself, now for her mother's sake, and now, when he was specially bitter, for her own.

'She certainly believed you dead,' said Lady Elizabeth. 'I do not suppose she knows that you are alive now. Her husband would probably not tell her, if even he knows; and I am sure Mrs. Clanricarde would not.'

'She *shall* know, that I swear!' said Charlie excitedly.

Caleb touched his arm with a deprecating hand.

'Would it not be better to let her live in peace?' he asked humbly. 'It is done now, and cannot be undone. Should she not be left to bear what she has to bear, without more being added to it?'

'That is my affair, not yours,' said Charlie haughtily, and the poor omadhaun for a moment shrank back.

Then, emboldened by his loyal love, and to spare her whom he loved the faintest thrill of pain, he said steadily:

'Not all your affair, Mr. Osborne. There is a right and a wrong to everything, and all who value another have a certain voice in their matters. We have the right to speak—both Lady Elizabeth and I—in a matter which touches the happiness of Mrs. Harford. For we are her friends too, as well as you, Mr. Osborne; though we have not your past; and we may without offence deprecate what would give her pain.'

It was scarcely Caleb Stagg who spoke. It was the hunchback whose wings were free and whose hump had gone.

'I shall do as I think best,' said Charlie proudly, unable to meet his former rival on this higher ground. 'Some day she shall know the infamous cheat that was practised on her, and shall recognize all of them, as the scoundrels they are. Father, mother, husband, friend—there was not one to warn her—not one to protect her!'

'Her friends did not know,' said Lady Elizabeth. 'I was not here;' and: 'It was evening post when I heard the news,' said Caleb.

'Among you you have broken my heart and

destroyed her life !' said Charlie with a burst of passion, as he turned abruptly away, feeling truly the Ishmaelite among men—his hand against every man's—every man's hand against his.

CHAPTER XVII.

THE HOME-COMING.

THE Harfords had been many months abroad. A strange instinct of danger kept Anthony out of England, loitering among Italian towns and Swiss châlets, where he had his beautiful young wife to himself, and where no rocks were ahead which he did not see. But few people knew of their whereabouts, and those few who did would not give the address to inconvenient inquirers. Mrs. Clanricarde, for instance, was safe, besides being very rarely written to ; while of all her friends and acquaintances in Kingshouse Estelle kept up a correspondence with none. Even Lady Elizabeth had been silently dropped, and Anthony did not wish things different from what they were. Jealous and exclusive, he disclaimed all sympathy with American ideas touching the freedom of women, and for his own part would, an' he could, have kept his treasure as the Afreet kept his—locked up from the gaze of all men, and sacred to himself alone.

For himself, he scarcely knew whether he was happy or not. Estelle had come back to her more normal state of being. She was no longer the dry, gloomy, and at times almost fierce recalcitrant that she had been in the beginning of her sorrow. She was gentle and compliant, and seemed to have accepted her position, with, at the least, patience. But something had gone from her. Some vitality of emotion had been quenched, which made her as apathetic as she was gentle—as dead as she was resigned. She never expressed a wish nor made an objection. To whatever her husband proposed she assented without a word of pleasure on the one hand, of suggestion on the other. If he wished to go or to stay it was all one to her; and whether he proposed Pontresina or Palermo, she was equally indifferent and equally compliant.

Sometimes, when he held her in his arms, Anthony felt as if he had married one of those mythical women of old romance—a being of appearance only, wanting the real life of humanity. She seemed to move as in a dream, with only half her faculties. No beauties of art nor of nature roused her to enthusiasm—made her laugh with joy or quiver with that sublimer delight which is so near akin to tears. She went through all the churches and all the picture-galleries, and assented to her husband's Philstinism as she would have assented to the most high-flown æstheticism. When he stigmatized the pre-Raffælites, the Francias and Giottos and the rest, as no better than a redskin's craft, she said 'No' quite meekly. Had he raved in Ruskinese of their supreme gloriousness and immortality she would have said ' Yes ' just as indifferently. She saw nothing that he did not point out to her, and when she did see it she did not take it in.

So they wandered over Europe, and Anthony

did his best to warm this lovely statue into life and re-animate the dead heart with a new love. It was all in vain. He poured out the treasures of his own love to utter futility. It was like bathing in his life's blood the marble feet of that fated Arabian prince. He might bathe them as he would, he could not make them warm or other than marble! Still, he would not despair. He believed in time and its power of working miracles, and he thought that no woman born of man could for ever resist such love as his—so patient, so strong, so devoted as it was. He would wait and he would not despair. Some day the divine spark would be given, and then his lovely statue would throb into life upon his breast. Some day that must be; and he could afford to wait.

Meanwhile, his hope had another source. When her child should be born—their child—that would perhaps rouse up in her a freer activity of feeling. For the sake of this new treasure she would love him who had given it to her, and the passion of maternity would double back on itself and create the wifely. He watched over her with a tenderness, a solicitude, equalling that of the fondest mother. Had she been sufficiently alive to feel anything at all, he would have stifled her with his care—he would have irritated and oppressed her. As it was, she accepted it all with her sweet, mechanical, unmeaning smile, and thanked him by the pure instinct of good breeding and her natural grace. And he—he would not see how that smile was simply mechanical, how that courtesy was merely instinctive. His own love created hers according to his own fancy; and with this he made himself content.

Anthony would have stayed still longer abroad had it not been for this expected birth. He had not much intellectual impedimenta in the way of sentiment, but what he had he cherished and held by. He wished his child to be born at Thrift. His son, who had to inherit, must see the light of day at his own ancestral home; for, like the French Emperor, he had settled the sex beforehand in his own mind, and it was as if he had commanded Nature to obey his will in this as in other things. Hence, they had to come home, while Estelle had still strength enough for the journey.

'You will like to be at your own home?' her husband said.

He had her hands in one of his, with his other he smoothed her curling jet-black hair.

She smiled in her usual way. Her hands were perfectly passive in his; her head, a little drooped forward, neither bent to his touch nor turned from it.

'Yes, if you wish it,' she said.

'And you?'

'Yes.'

'You like Thrift? You remember how beautiful it looked last year in the early spring, even though not then in its full beauty? You remember that avenue of chestnuts just bursting into leaf?'

'Thrift?' said Estelle, with a puzzled look. 'What avenue?'

'My darling!' laughed Anthony; 'don't you remember the avenue there, where you and I walked one day after we were engaged, and I made you kiss me under the old beech-tree? Have you forgotten?'

A shudder like the shivering of strong fever came over Estelle.

'Oh!' she said, as if in pain; 'don't! don't!'

'Have I hurt you?' he asked tenderly, releasing her hands. 'Did I hurt you by too hard a pressure?'

For all answer Estelle covered her face as if against some painful sight, still shivering, but not weeping, not sobbing—only once a slight moan, as of some one in suppressed pain, showing that she suffered.

'What have I done, Estelle?' asked Anthony, always in anxious fear.

She made no answer. She did not seem to hear him. Nor indeed did she. Her mind and faculties were swept away in that one bitter flood of remembrance when she had fully realized the step she had taken, and been forced to give that caress to her master and her future husband. It was a paroxysm like to what she had never known since she had married—when this mortal deadness of the soul had settled down on her, and she had existed in quiescence because only half alive.

But it passed as all things do, and she came back to her more usual self. Paroxysms are necessarily transient, and there was no use in kicking against the pricks! Charlie was dead; she was married; in a few weeks now she would be a mother—and she had to live for the sake of others if not for her own. She made some lame kind of excuse, which in its way satisfied Anthony and soothed him—partly because he wished to be satisfied and was eager to be soothed. And things went on after this little outbreak as they had gone before—in the same quiescence from her and the same tender solicitous and ceaseless care from him.

Then the home-journey was made, and they came back to England and soon were re-established at Thrift. They had no demonstrative home-coming—no parade of tenantry nor of school-children—no triumphal arches nor bonfires. Quietly, as Anthony loved to do all things, and unobtrusively, as was Estelle's way, they took up their abode at his old home, where even

Mr. and Mrs. Clanricarde had not been asked to receive them. They came, however, in a few days after the arrival; and Estelle received them just in the same spirit as that in which she used to go through the Italian galleries and look at the palaces and churches. She was neither glad nor sorry, neither excited nor displeased. When they came to the station, where she and Anthony had driven to meet them, she kissed her mother as if she had seen her yesterday—her father perhaps felt a shade more warmth in her tepid caress. She did not remark on their appearance, nor ask of the old friends at Kingshouse—she made her mother comfortable in the carriage, and then left the talking to her and Anthony. When spoken to she smiled, and answered as if with a certain effort of will to collect her thoughts and focus her attention, relapsing into silence the instant she had said her allotted say. But she was not actively unhappy, and she looked in good health—as indeed she was. And with this her parents had to be content. For that finer subtler something else which had been killed in her, that had to go—the main things had been secured.

'Do you not think she is looking splendidly well?' asked Anthony of his mother-in-law, when they stood for a moment together in the embrasure of the window, and looked out on the noble park and stately gardens which his love and her diplomacy had secured for Estelle.

'Splendid,' she replied. 'You have taken good care of her, Anthony.'

'As of my life!' he said with fervour. 'She is more than my life to me.'

'She ought to be a happy girl to have secured so good a husband,' returned Mrs. Clanricarde with a smile, flattering, caressing, like the purring of a cat when she rubs herself against your knee.

'She is,' said Anthony emphatically. 'How should she not be? She has everything that human being can want, and I love her.'

He said this with an accent of pride that was almost fierce; but underneath was a certain want of sincerity and desire to assure himself, which Mrs. Clanricarde was astute enough to catch.

‘Yes, indeed,’ she said with the same purring kind of manner. ‘As you say, it would be impossible not to be happy with all that you have given her—all that you have done for her. And I know her so well. I know what a tender, grateful, responsive nature hers is.’

Anthony’s face changed. An expression came over it that was not pleasant to see. Mrs. Clanricarde’s assurances burnt in him like fire passing over a wound. His own inner convictions he could bear and stifle, resolutely binding them down as a man deals with wild beasts; but when it came to this woman touching that inner sore and prophesying smooth things where smooth things were not, then he writhed under the pain, and felt as if he could have strangled her there as she stood.

We are all conscious of the falsehood with which we live, striving to believe it truth. We do not look in the face of the lie all day long and see nothing else; but we are vaguely conscious of it always, and sometimes we are acutely possessed by the sorrow it brings with it. As now with Anthony. It was hard work to bear up under the truth. He knew that he had not won Estelle. For all his love and care, his passionate desire to gain her heart, his eager devotion, his very fever of endeavour to win her, he knew that he had not caught one single ray of her affection. She endured him because she was obliged to endure him—because she had no alternative, no place of refuge from him ; because, too, she was of a sweet and gentle nature and she could not belie herself. But she only endured him on these lines of compulsion. She did not love him ; she did not care for him so much as she would have cared for a dog that had been hallowed by her old lover's hand. She was utterly and profoundly indifferent to him at her best moments, and she revolted with her whole being at her worst.

All this he knew, as he knew that one day he must die and be buried. But he tried to forget it ; and sometimes did—and to bear it with manful courage and loving hope ; as also he did. Yet Mrs. Clanricarde must not touch that sore, and pretend that things were other than what they were—that Estelle was loving and responsive when she was dead and inert.

The clear eyes of the clever diplomatist saw the whole situation at a glance. She could not recall her words, and she could not show Anthony that she had read his heart; but in the easiest and most graceful way possible she added, as an afterthought: 'At present she is a little languid, and, indeed, I might almost say, apathetic; but that will pass when her child is born. I have often seen young mothers expectant like this.'

Then Anthony's stern bronzed face brightened. Here was an intelligible basis for hope —a material foothold that he could stand on.

'Yes,' he said. 'I suppose so. She is not, as you say, Mrs. Clanricarde, very lively just at present, but I suppose it will pass. Indeed, I am sure it will.'

'So am I,' said Estelle's mother briskly, just as her daughter came slowly towards her, saying: 'Will you not go to your room, mother?' as if she had said: 'Two and two make four,' with no more emphasis and no more animation.

'Her mind is certainly touched!' said Mrs. Clanricarde to herself, as she went upstairs. 'What a dreadful thing, and in her state, too! Pray heaven she may never know that this detestable young man is alive! If she finds it out—well, there will be a catastrophe, that is very certain! And the blame will fall on me. It always does fall on the mother when a good marriage turns out ill!'

CHAPTER XVIII.

THE SPIDER AND THE FLY.

HOPE'S tales were false and flattering, as usual. Estelle's new state of motherhood left her general condition unchanged. Naturally, she loved the child ; but she took no more interest than before in anything else. And she loved the child in an odd manner—with a jealousy, a fitfulness, utterly foreign to her former character. Once when the nurse, thinking to please her with the inane chatter considered good enough for young mothers, said that this red little bundle of flannel and potentialities was like its bronzed and sinewy father, Estelle put the creature back into her arms with visible annoyance, and would not look at it for hours after.

As she grew stronger in health her apathy seemed to increase. She cared nothing for her duties as house-mistress and local suzerain, and did not fulfil them. The house kept itself between her maid and the cook; and she neither knew nor noticed how things went. Society eddied round her in balls and dinners, tennis-parties and afternoons, according to its wont. She seldom went where invited, and she would not invite in return. She appeared to read as much as if she had been a sincere student, but as often as not her book was upside down, and she would sit for hours without turning a page. Sometimes she took up a length of embroidery, but she seldom got beyond the first few stitches, and these she did as often wrongly as not. When Anthony spoke to hers he answered him always in the same gentle way of bare and brief response, which left him nothing to complain of save its lifelessness and want of spontaneity. She never contradicted him nor opposed him, but she never went before his wish with a suggestion of her own, and she neither looked at him when she spoke to him nor returned his caresses. The only thing that seemed to stir her to activity of feeling was when he touched the child. Then her soft brown eyes became dark and gloomy as with suppressed indignation, and her pallid face would flush as if her veins were living fire. But even to this she did not openly object, much as it cost her to endure what she felt as desecration ; and her self-control at such moments was the most conscious act of her apparently stagnant and unconscious mind. But if anyone could have opened that window in her breast through which her thoughts could be read, what a wild world would have been revealed!—what mad and feverish plans of escape with her child to some unknown and distant land where she could live with him and her fatal memories, and forget the hideous slavery into which she had been sold! She had always on her person that money so mysteriously sent to Charlie. Viewed by the light of her desires it was a bank that would never fail—a river of gold that would never run dry. If only she could escape from England, and put Thrift, her husband, and her hated name for ever behind her! What a volcano raged and burnt beneath that soft, still, frozen cover! What a very fierceness of hatred was masked by that gentle sweetness and that unresponsive apathy! And how well she kept the secret of her heart, and how perfectly she played her part!

What Anthony suffered, felt, or thought, no one knew, and perhaps he scarcely confessed to himself. Nothing could exceed, little could equal, his exquisite tenderness—his strong and patient forbearance. He wearied himself with devising how to interest and amuse his pale and unresponsive wife. He gave her rich presents, which she accepted with a forced smile and feeble thanks, looked at once, then put away and never looked at again. He proposed excursions, to which she assented, and whence she returned as she had gone, like a person half-asleep whose eyes had taken in nothing of all they had seen. He read to her, and she did not know whether what he had read were prose or poetry, nor what the subject nor the story. Yet his love survived all this bitter regimen of drought and starvation; and he sought ever more and more strenuously to win her—to force open that closed door of her heart and to establish himself there as its cherished inmate. He would not confess that he was baffled, and that he was as far from her love as he had been from the beginning. Yet, day by day, he grew leaner, graver, more morose to others, more irritable, more dangerous to meddle with or to cross—to her only and to the child showing grace or tenderness. With his heart's blood he watered the desert sands which gave him back nothing in return. There was not even the humblest little flower of love—there was nothing but barren sand and lifeless rock.

Closely surrounded as she was by this investing love, Estelle had little or no freedom. Only on the days when Anthony was forced to attend to his magisterial duties had she the sense of comparative liberty and the feeling of release from a companionship that was as oppressive as jailerdom—a surveillance which, however loving it might be, she secretly resented and chafed under. For, indeed, if Anthony had loved her less things would have been better between them. But his love was too strong for her. It stifled her as much as a gazelle is stifled in the folds of a python; and the very means he took to win were those which further estranged her. Had he left her more alone her repugnance would have been at least less active, and she would not have hated her life with so much inner heat. But when will the unloved learn that to woo the reluctant beloved is to kill, not create—and that the most passionate kisses ever rained by the living on a corpse will not bring that corpse to life, though the living die in the effort?

One day Anthony went to a rather distant town where he had to sit, judging cases, and whence he was sure not to return till night. Estelle had never been to see Mrs. Latimer or her servant—Charlie Osborne's former nurse—since that day when she had gone with her father and mother and Anthony, then only her lover. She had often thought of these two people, with whom the outer edge of her life's greater circle so strangely touched, but she had had no power to go there again. Before the birth of her child the walk had been too far for her; she would not have proposed a visit to her husband; and she did not choose to take the carriage. She did not want the servants to know that she had gone. To-day the opportunity seemed ready-made to her hand. Her husband was out for the day; she had recovered her strength, and could walk now as she used. The weather was perfect; and her aching heart was always full of the one love—the one memory—with no room for any other, save that newly-discovered tract where her child had laid its little hand. Accordingly, she walked across the park and down Meads-lane, till she came to that row of houses standing on the outskirts of the town and at the extremity of the Thrift estate, in one of which Mrs. Latimer and Mary Crosby lived in their strict seclusion and by no means overcharged luxury. Estelle knocked at the door, and Mary, after scanning her in the mirror set edgewise against the window, went back to the old lady, and said in an excited whisper:

'Glory! it's Mrs. Harford at last! Pull down

the blind, Mrs. Latimer, muffle up your head, and keep the room dark. We can do with her. It's the Lord's mercy she has come!'

Then she went to the door, which she opened with a face as composed and a manner as set as if she did not know whom to expect. When she saw Estelle, that face broke into smiles as eloquent as caresses—smiles which warmed the poor dead heart as nothing had done for all these weary months of pain and loss.

'Well, Mary! How glad I am to see you again!' said Estelle, shaking hands impulsively with Charlie's old nurse.

How fast she must have walked! Her face was crimson, and her breathing rapid. One would have said she had run the last half of the way.

'And I am glad to see you, Miss Estelle,' said Mary, answering back that friendly impulsiveness with its kind. 'Come in, miss—lor, deary me!—Mrs. Harford, I should have said. But one forgets. Mrs. Latimer is in one of her better ways to-day. She'll likely be able to see you. She will if she can, that I know; for I have talked a great deal to her of old times, when I was Master Charlie's nurse and you and he were children together. I know she will see you if she can. So come in, please.'

'Thank you; yes, I will,' said Estelle, who had quivered at the old familiar name.

Her wistful eyes were fastened on the clear-cut resolute face above her. She was conscious of but one feeling rather than thought. Mary had held Charlie in her arms; Mary had loved him; he had loved her. She had cared for him and tended him with even more zeal than she herself cared for and tended her own little child. On her rested the reflection of the past glory; and she felt that Mary lived in her dead love, and knew that she would sympathize with her, if she were told all, as no other human being did or could. She stood nearer to her than mother, father, husband, child—this resolute woman of the people, who had been Charlie Osborne's nurse.

The woman read to the faintest line the face that looked into hers with such a passion of sorrow. She was one of those shrewd mental detectives who see clearly, because not blinded by fanciful theories of impracticable virtues and impossible crimes. To Mary Crosby all frailties were possible; and, unlike the more delicate handling of Mrs. Clanricarde, she did not lament the tattered condition of the phœnix bird's tail feathers—she did not believe in the phœnix bird at all. She took Estelle into the state drawing-room—the same room into which she had been taken on that former visit more than a year ago. And Mary saw how the young wife shuddered as the memory of that day came back on her mind.

' If I don't make something of this!' thought Mary, feeling like one tapping all round a cabinet to find the secret drawer with its hidden key.

' I will go and see if Mrs. Latimer can see you, miss—Mrs. Harford,' she then said, with a perceptible hesitation on the name. Why did she want to recall her unmarried state to Estelle? What ailed her, as the Scotch say, at her present condition as the wife of Mrs. Latimer's landlord? Had Estelle been in full possession of her natural mind she would have seen these ominous little threads, and would have feared them ; but she was too pre-occupied to see anything but her own inner self, or to be conscious of aught but her own sorrowful thoughts.

In a short time Mary came back. Yes ; Mrs. Latimer was well enough to see her to-day. She was only poorly at the best of times, but she was in her bettermore way to-day—the Lord be thanked!—for Mary Crosby was devout as well as devoted—as good a Christian as she was an attached servant. On which, Estelle accompanied Charlie's old nurse into the back room, where, sitting in the dim obscurity of a darkened chamber, muffled up in shawls and buried in pillows, sat the tenacious old annuitant, whose ugly trick of living was keeping the Clanricardes out of a tidy little income sorely needed, while adding a few unexpected plums to poor Charlie Osborne's not too luscious loaf.

'This is Miss Clanricarde, ma'am, as was, Mrs. Harford as is,' shouted Mary to the old lady. 'She is that deaf,' she added in a natural voice to Estelle.

' Glad to see you, ma'am,' said the old lady, coughing lugubriously.

' I am sorry you have such a cough,' said tender-hearted Estelle, far more alive to things here than she was at her own home—far more interested in outside matters and persons than her husband had known her through all those unsatisfactory months.

' Hey? what does she say?' asked Mrs. Latimer of Mary.

Mary repeated the phrase in her boatswain's voice, and Mrs. Latimer was made to hear.

' It is my grave-cough, my dear,' she answered. ' Your father will soon come into my little bit of money. I'm not long for this world, I can tell you, and the Lord will soon have mercy on my old bones.'

' I hope not so bad as that,' said Estelle, with genuine sympathy in response to the false appeal—as has been the way of the world ever since the serpent put on the child's face and looked at Eve from among the branches of the apple-tree.

The old woman's keen black eyes twinkled.

'Lord love your dear innocent heart!' she said, and coughed more vigorously than before.

'Best not let her talk, Mrs. Harford,' then interposed Mary. 'Talking makes her cough so bad! And you see she is an old lady now and rambles a good deal. She has only half her senses, as a body might say. Blind and deaf, and sleeps away half her time, and rambles on like winking the other half. She is bad to do with at times, is the poor old lady, and so I tell you. But I do my duty by her, miss, and shall to the end—your mother may be sure of that. I do my duty by her, and let her want for nothing.

'I am sure of that,' said Estelle, looking at Mary with her soft eyes full of love and the inner light of memory. 'I remember how good you always were.'

'To poor dear Master Charlie?'

'Yes,' said Estelle, with a quiver in her voice.

'Ah, but then I loved him! Who would not?' said Mary. 'He was the very bonniest little lad and the dearest young gentleman as ever wore shoe-leather. I never knew his equal!'

'Nor I,' said Estelle, with the frankness of despair.

There was no reason why she should not carry this incense of fidelity to that dear grave —why she should not keep his memory like a perfume in her heart.

'That was a queer start, that word of his death, was it not, Miss Estelle—Mrs. Harford, I mean?' asked Mary.

Estelle opened her eyes. They were full of tears.

'Why?' she asked in her turn. 'What was there queer in it?'

'Why, did you not know?' said Mary in surprise. 'It was false news. He is not dead at all. The back-word came into the paper, let me see, the twenty-sixth of April, last year— yes, the twenty-sixth of April. And now this is August, a year gone, and we have heard no more about him.'

Estelle started up from her place as if she had been struck. Her face was white and rigid;

her eyes were dark and strained; her parted lips were as full of horror as a Greek tragic mask. She looked as if suddenly turned to stone, but with always the fiery heart of suffering within the marble body.

'The twenty-sixth of April—last year,' she said slowly.

'Yes, ma'am,' answered Mary. 'I have it here.'

She opened a drawer in the table and took out a *Times* newspaper.

'There,' she said, pointing to the 'agony column,' 'there is Master Charlie's own words.'

Overcome, beside herself, like one distraught, Estelle read the words, which she carried to her lips with a low cry of mingled joy and pain, then fell prone on the floor as if she had been shot through the heart.

'Now the road's clear,' said Mary, as she lifted her up and dashed cold water in her face. 'It is as plain as daylight, and I was right. They've sold the poor young thing to this man here, and she loves Master Charlie as a wife shouldn't ought. There is a bad day in store for Mr.

Harford and the rest of them ; and I reckon I've got pepper enough for them now if they come nosing about us any more.'

'My word, Mary, but you are bold !' said Mrs. Latimer, as she had so often said before. Her admiration of the younger woman's cleverness and audacity increased rather than diminished with each fresh manifestation.

'What I put my hand to I don't turn back from,' said Mary sententiously, as she still busied herself about Estelle.

At last the girl came out of her swoon and re-entered the thorny path of consciousness. She could not now, if even she would, deny the confession she had involuntarily made. Nature had forced her secret from her, and the torn veil could not be replaced. Mary knew her heart, and so far held her in the hollow of her hand. But she did not think of this in the light of danger to herself. She thought only of the woman's sympathy, so certain because of her own love for Charlie. She would be pitiful to her— understanding how another should also love him, even though that other were now a wife and mother. And she would be some one to whom she, Estelle, could come and talk without fear or stint. Whenever there was a free day she would come over to Highstile Lane and talk to Mary Crosby of Charlie—Charlie, the child whom she had nursed—Charlie, the man whom Estelle still loved. But the black wickedness of those who should have been her best friends— the cruelty of those who should have cared for her and protected her! She saw it all, as clearly as she saw the words themselves. Her mother had inserted the lie of Charlie's death that the way might be free for Anthony. The marriage had been hastened on with such indecent hurry that the contradiction might not arrive meanwhile. It had come on the very day, and it had been kept from her. At the altar itself she would have turned back and refused to become Anthony's wife had she known that Charlie was still alive. Hoodwinked, betrayed, entrapped, what faith did she owe to any of them? What right had they to her life? None! From this moment she felt herself essentially free. The past had been before the present, and her very child had not the claim that Charlie Osborne had.

The wakening from those long months of mental lethargy and emotional dreaming had come with a vengeance! Burning with fever, strong with the fictitious strength of mingled outrage and despair—the armour in which her love had clothed itself—Estelle felt as if she could have braved the whole world for the sake of the one dear love of her life. All she wanted now was to see him, to hear his voice, to tell him how her heart had been broken, how her life had been ruined by the shameful lie which had been palmed off on her for truth; but how through it all she had kept her love and her faith and constancy substantially intact. They had sold her body into worse than Egyptian bondage, but they had not touched her soul, her love, her heart. All that she had been she still was; and the love that had grown with her growth and had lived through all opposition was still as pure and true as when they last met and parted.

Ay! pure and true, for all that hated ring on her finger and that alien babe at her breast !

Full of these thoughts she went back through the park to the house she had never adopted as her home. But, like all timid creatures, she knew that she must hide what she felt, if she could not feign what she did not feel.   And when Anthony came home he found her as he had left her— silent, quiescent, unresponsive, monosyllabic— neither pleased with nor averse from—a mere sweet and patient living corpse, whose love he poured out his strong heart's blood in vain to win. But he noticed with the quick eyes of love that her hands burnt as if with fever, that her usually pale face was flushed and hectic, and that her parched lips were dry. He noticed, too, when he took her in his arms and drew her to his breast with that tenderness, that infinite yearning of the unloved seeking to gain what is denied, that she visibly shuddered and drew herself away as if she had been stung. He did not let her see what pain this mute repulse gave him. As gently, as tenderly as he had taken her did he now relinquish her; but over all his inner being came the deadly sickness which men call despair—that anguish of impotent fury which would revenge itself if it could, and which cannot find the object.

CHAPTER XIX.

LIKE A BIRD TO ITS NEST.

CHARLIE, still lingering at Kingshouse, took that strange pleasure so much indulged in by the sorrowful of adding to his distress of mind by every means in his power. He went over all the old walks and lived again in the past delusive pleasures. He was never weary of handling the skeleton and making it dance like one of Holbein's Deaths; of uncovering the grave and looking at the face of the corpse; of turning the knife in his wound. He was indefatigable in self-torture; and being already in weak bodily health, he made himself worse by all this unnecessary mental fever and fretting. Every one pitied him, so pale and hollow-eyed, so gaunt and sad as he was; and every one prophesied for him a speedy rest beneath the peaceful sods of the churchyard.

Even Mrs. Clanricarde found a compassionate corner in her heart for the enemy whom she had disabled. She wished that she could have secured her own release from debt, and Estelle's sufficient establishment, by less painful methods than her daughter's life-long misery and Charlie Osborne's threatened dissolution. It was very sad; but then people are so headstrong and unreasonable, and will not see things as they are, nor act rationally! What business had these two young people to fall in love as they had done? They knew the thing was impossible. It was their folly, not her falsehood, which had wrought all this mischief; and we must be responsible, each of us, for our own doings.

Nevertheless, she was sorry to see the poor boy looked so ill, and wished that she could have comforted him. But Charlie would have none of her sympathy; and Mrs. Clanricarde, with a French shrug of her shoulders, left him to his fate and called him 'impayable'—in which mysterious word she seemed to find boundless satisfaction. To be able to cast a stone when one has done all the wrong is such a pleasure to the wrong-doer, slinging his pebble afield.

One sultry summer's day a letter came to Charlie Osborne—an anonymous letter, in the well-known handwriting, but with a different postmark. Hitherto all these letters had been posted in London; but this was stamped Thorbergh. It contained money and these words :

'Come to Thorbergh. You are badly wanted. Your old nurse, Mary Crosby, lives at 3, Highstile Lane, and can tell you some things you ought to know.'

Thorbergh ! the place where his faithless love had her home. What new delusion was this? What meshes were enclosing him ? And who was his unknown friend who sent him these sporadic supplies ? It could not be she, for they had come to him before her great wealth had come to her. It could not be Mary Crosby herself. How could a poor servant send him money far exceeding any possible wages or savings she might have? Yet the handwriting was the same; and the money was sent in the same way as that to which he had been accustomed of late years; and the triple connection of Thorbergh, Estelle, and Mary Crosby was clear.

He tossed through the night, wondering, pondering, and never divining; and when morning came he had not made up his mind what it were best to do—whether he should go and learn for himself the meaning of the mystery, or leave it alone as perhaps a snare—perhaps a deception.

Then his thoughts shifted. Was Estelle unhappy? Did she want him to help her, to defend her, to avenge her? Was she less sinning than sinned against? Had she been forced into this shameful union, after having been deceived into believing it no crime to a living lover—no infraction of a vital vow? These thoughts thronged and burned till they convinced him. He saw neither danger nor possible fraud in the letter which called him to the place where Estelle lived. He saw only that she was in need of him to defend her against her husband—which was, as comparing himself to Anthony Harford, as if a nightingale were to protect a linnet against a hawk. That, however, he did not stop to consider. The calculation of relatives touching strength and power was outside present conditions. Wherefore, by the afternoon he had his portmanteau packed, and was off to Thorbergh to question Mary Crosby, whose name had got so strangely mixed up in his affairs, and learn from her, if he could, the meaning of this mysterious summons.

The next day, as early as was practicable, Charlie found the house where Mrs. Latimer lived in such strict seclusion; and was welcomed by Mary with shrill exclamations of wonderment and delight. She had never expected to see him again, she said—with the familiarity of old affection holding his hand in one of hers, while she placed the other on his shoulder. When she had seen his death in the paper she had been that grieved she could not say! She had put black into her bonnet and worn a black gown ever onwards till she had seen the contradiction, and then she felt as if she must have danced in white! She did not look, however, to see him again. How should she? What did he know of her, nor where she was, nor how she was doing, nor aught about her anyhow? No; she did not expect to see him this side of the grave, and she had put all her hope and trust into meeting him in heaven. And then she wiped her eyes with her apron, as servants do, and Charlie felt his heart go out to this hard-featured woman who had been his nurse, and who certainly had done her duty by him when she had had it to do.

He went into the cold, hard, primly-set best drawing-room, and there began his cross-examination. He showed Mary the letter he had received, and asked her what she knew about it.

'Nay, what,' she said in answer, 'I know nought at all! If it were the last word I had to speak I'd say it with my dying breath. I know nought about it anyway.'

'But what have you to tell me?' he asked

again. 'Why should I be summoned here?'

'That caps me,' said Mary. 'That's just what gets over me, Master Charlie.'

Charlie thought for an instant before speaking. His eyes were turned to the floor; Mary's were on his face.

'Do you remember Miss Clanricarde?' he then asked with a certain reluctance. He did not like to bring her name into the vulgar light of a servant's quasi-confidence.

'Mrs. Harford as is?' she returned. 'Yes, I know her well. Mr. Harford is the landlord of all this lot. He is Mrs. Latimer's landlord; and Mrs. Harford sometimes comes to see us.'

Poor Charlie's face changed as eloquently as Estelle's when she had heard of his continued existence. He covered his eyes with his hand. The mystery deepened, but the glory that shone through its darkness blinded him. Could it have been she herself who had sent the letter? But no! the handwriting was familiar. It was connected with those sporadic supplies, and these were not connected with her. No; it was not Estelle who had summoned him, and not Mary Crosby. Who, in heaven's name, could it be?

'Mrs. Harford was here only the other day,' continued Mary in an indifferent voice. 'She had not heard of your being alive, Master Charlie—as I am that glad to see. She had not heard of it till I chanced to tell her.'

'No?' said Charlie with a shout. 'And then?'

'Well, you see, sir, the shock was almost too much for her,' continued Mary. 'She is in poor health, poor young lady, and looks white and thin—as white and thin as yourself, Master Charlie. And when I showed her the paper, why, she just skriked and fainted, even end on the floor. You were always like brother and sister, I remember, so she was bound to be upset—and I should have remembered me in time.'

Charlie got up and walked to the window. His heart was beating wildly, his eyes were dim, his head was dizzy. She loved him, then; loved him now as much as ever; and her marriage had been as he had always believed—forgetting the baser whisperings of his angry suspicions

—a forced marriage founded on a lie. She was faithful to him still. Dear, sweet, loving and beloved Estelle !—faithful, faithful for life and to death—as he to her !

And now, what was to be done? He was here and she was not an hour's walk apart. He was in the very room of which she had breathed the air only so short a time ago. He seemed to feel the fragrance of the flowers she had worn, to see the glory of the light she had brought with her. He was in her neighbourhood, close to her.   A turn in the road and they might meet. All Thorbergh was filled with her potential presence, and Charlie felt as if he should not be able to rest nor sleep nor shelter in the house lest he should lose the chance of meeting her. He was here and she was not an hour's walk apart ; and yet, were they not separated as completely as though impassable mountains and the unharvested sea lay between them ?   They were, in fact, farther apart than when he had been sick with fever in Yokohama, and she had been free and unfettered at Kings- house.

But they must meet. He must see her, cost what it might. He owed nothing to the man who had robbed him of her; nothing to the society, the superstition, which sanctioned this sacrilege and called it sacred. He owed himself only to her, to clear himself from any possible charge of indifference, carelessness, wrongdoing anyhow. He owed himself only to her.

He stood in the prim-set parlour of the house where he had thought to find the heart of the mystery, but had not—his brain seething and his blood boiling; while Mary watched him, and felt as a chess-player feels when he has made a masterly move which protects his threatened king so that no attack can stand.

'Does Mrs. Harford often come here?' then asked Charlie, when he came back to himself so far as to remember that he owed something to appearances, and that Mary Crosby was not in his confidence.

'Not often, sir. Only when Mr. Harford is away,' was the answer. 'I fancy he keeps her pretty tight,' she added, as a compassionate coda or afterthought.

'Brute!' said Charlie with a groan.

'A little that way, I think,' said Mary with a sigh.

Charlie clenched his hands. If he could but have used them as battering-rams to pound the life out of that scoundrel!

'When was she last here?' he asked.

'Let me see—this is Friday. Last Monday— no, last Tuesday,' was the answer.

'And she will not be here again?'

'Not unless Mr. Harford leaves home for the day. Then maybe she will slip over here to have a talk of old times,' said Mary. 'She seems to look back a great deal,' she added. 'Ladies mostly do when they are not well suited.'

'I should like to see her again,' said Charlie, after a pause.

'Why not call, Master Charlie?' Mary asked innocently. 'I am certain sure she would be fain to see you. She is of the kind to love her own, and you are like her own—like her very brother, as one might say.'

'I do not know Mr. Harford; and I would

not care to call at his place,' said Charlie, a little reluctantly.

He was unfolding his heart more than he cared, and yet he could not keep it closed.

'No, I see,' said Mary, as demure as he was reluctant.

'Perhaps I shall meet her,' then said Charlie, moving towards the door. 'I should like to see her.'

'Yes, you'll be sure to meet her,' returned Mary cheerfully. 'Mr. Harford drives her a good deal about the country. You'll be main sure to meet them.'

'Confound and curse Mr. Harford!' cried Charlie, beside himself. 'For God's sake, Mary, spare me his name!'

'All right, sir. I have no particular affection for him myself,' was her answer. 'All the same, Miss Estelle is his wife, you see, Master Charlie, and a wife is bound to follow her husband's lead.'

'I will wring his neck!' groaned Charlie.

Mary looked as she used in olden times when he was naughty and had to be spanked.

'Oh fie! Master Charlie,' she said, in just the old tone of reproof. 'What has the poor gentleman done to you, I should like to know?'

'What no gentleman would have done—what a cur like him deserves hanging for!' shouted Charlie. 'He has taken the woman I love and who loves me—and he has taken her by a lie—and he knew it.'

Mary's face took on its natural hardness curves and lines of the softest sympathy.

'I am sorry! oh, my, I am that sorry!' she said, her apron to her eyes and her womanly sob quite audible. After a time she seemed to compose herself. 'Master Charlie,' she said, with the straightness of a sudden thought, 'why do you not come here to stay, rather than to the hotel? There is plenty of room here, and I could do for you fine. Why not send your luggage here? You could then stay as long as you liked in Thorbergh, and no one be a penny the worse or wiser. We live that quiet, no one sees or knows what passes here. You, and even more than you, could have the best bedroom and this parlour, and you'd be as safe as if locked up in a church. If you'd like it, Master Charlie, think of it. You'll find me as good as my word.'

'God bless you, Mary! my dear, good Mary!' was the poor young fellow's reply, as, impulsively, he put his arm round her waist and kissed her as in his boyish days.

Some vague feeling that this offer might serve him in good stead filled his heart with hope and light. He did not know what he thought—he did not formulate nor arrange his feelings into words—but he felt that he had a hiding-place if he wanted it. And perhaps he might.

With another burst of thanks to this servant of the tough old annuitant, he promised to bring his portmanteau that evening at dark—to bring it himself, no one knowing where he went; and then he left the house and took the road up Mead's-lane, with full directions from Mary where to find the park and grounds of Thrift.

More mad than sane, Charlie walked on with but one hope, one desire, one intention. He would see her again. The mystery of his summons ceased to interest him. The source whence those pleasant little golden showers fell on him also ceased to interest him. He forgot Mary and all that life contained, save that one lodestar of his love—that glorious and beloved Estelle. He would see her again. He would hear from her own lips the story of her sorrow and their sin. He would hold her in his arms and clasp her to his heart. She was his. She was not this man's—this border ruffian, this gambler, this horse-stealer, this rude, rough miner with one hand on his revolver and the other on a secreted card. There was not one of all the ruffians extant—from Jem Bludso to Jack Oakhurst—to whom Charlie did not mentally liken Anthony Harford—the man who had stolen Estelle from him, and was breaking his own heart because he could not win hers.

Always in this turmoil of tempestuous sorrow and longing Charlie went through the leafy lane till he came to a narrow opening between two uprights which led into a park. He passed through and walked on, knowing well enough where he was. He went on and on, walking always more rapidly, till he came to the gate of the private gardens surrounding a stately mansion, with an upper terrace leading down by a double flight of steps into the lower grounds. On this upper terrace stood a woman, dressed for walking. She was alone. Charlie came up the drive till he was near enough to see the face and figure clearly. It was Estelle—looking far away over the gardens and the park to the distant Beyond—there, where Charlie Osborne was somewhere to be found. She was too much absorbed in her own thoughts to see the man walking in the shadow of the trees towards the house. He came close under the terrace-wall, and then he called her by her name. She heard him, and bent over the parapet above, as one who had expected him—as one who had been waiting for this moment.

'Estelle!' he said. 'My darling! My beloved!'

With the old light eager tread—the old suggestion of a bird running to its nest—she ran down the steps and into the shadow of the wall, where—forgetting husband, child, her name of wife, her fair fame, and all the present

save that she was his—she flung herself into
her old lover's arms, and sobbed out

LONDON: PRINTED BY DUNCAN MACDONALD, BLENHEIM HOUSE.

www.ingramcontent.com/pod-product-compliance
Lightning Source LLC
Chambersburg PA
CBHW031038120726
47905CB00007B/2231